Tyrone Dines was born in 1962, the year Z-cars aired on the BBC and the Cuban missile crisis happened, although he says none of these events are linked to his birth.

Raised in rural Buckinghamshire, he occasionally went to school. Found work as varied as a truck driver, diver, and finally a suspension technician, he's travelled extensively, and now lives in the mountains in Northern Italy with his wife, Giulia, and their miniature wolf, Maisy.

This is his first published work.

This book is dedicated to my wife, Giulia, who is the source of calm in my chaotic world.

Tyrone Dines

THE WRITING ON THE MIRROR

AUSTIN MACAULEY PUBLISHERS
LONDON · CAMBRIDGE · NEW YORK · SHARJAH

Copyright © Tyrone Dines 2025

The right of Tyrone Dines to be identified as author of this work has been asserted by the author in accordance with sections 77 and 78 of the Copyright, Designs and Patents Act 1988.

All rights reserved. No part of this publication may be reproduced, stored in a retrieval system, or transmitted in any form or by any means, electronic, mechanical, photocopying, recording, or otherwise, without the prior permission of the publishers.

Any person who commits any unauthorised act in relation to this publication may be liable to criminal prosecution and civil claims for damages.

This is a work of fiction. Names, characters, businesses, places, events, locales, and incidents are either the products of the author's imagination or used in a fictitious manner. Any resemblance to actual persons, living or dead, or actual events is purely coincidental.

A CIP catalogue record for this title is available from the British Library.

ISBN 9781035879540 (Paperback)
ISBN 9781035879557 (ePub e-book)

www.austinmacauley.com

First Published 2025
Austin Macauley Publishers Ltd®
1 Canada Square
Canary Wharf
London
E14 5AA

Table of Contents

Chapter 1: Visual Reference	9
Chapter 2: Warm and Fuzzy	15
Chapter 3: The Smoke	23
Chapter 4: Stage Fright	34
Chapter 5: Clear	48
Chapter 6: Gathering	59
Chapter 7: Hello, Daddy	72
Chapter 8: Well, I Never	84
Chapter 9: Time	93
Chapter 10: Moments	106
Chapter 11: Message	118
Chapter 12: Mummy	133
Chapter 13: Grimaldi	147
Chapter 14: Hiding in Plain Sight	159
Chapter 15: Bits and Bangs	167
Chapter 16: Farm Life	180

Chapter 17: Boss?	**193**
Chapter 18: Dog Van	**205**
Chapter 19: Final	**219**

Chapter 1
Visual Reference

Adding another angle; he'd looked at it several different ways, but no matter how many times he tried to reference what he was seeing, it didn't seem to add up.

The way he'd looked at it, was it a trick of the light? It didn't seem so, it was real enough. By laying on the path he'd looked again; no, it stayed just as it was. Getting up just made him feel lightheaded; the effect of the amount of weed he'd smoked, the Guinness and the Jack Daniels, mixed, was really starting to kick in.

No, he didn't want to go and look any closer. Having looked at it several times, he'd now worked out that it looked fucking dangerous!

It was definitely much colder than before; the Converse All-Stars, jeans, a t-shirt and a Harrington jacket were probably not the wisest choice of clothing for a mid-January night. The pub had been super warm and the amount of people added to a mix of smells and atmosphere. Cigarette smoke, beer, a heady mix of perfume, hairspray, and the odd whiff of BO. Why the fuck was it that some folks really stink?

No, the cold was real. But that wasn't as such the concern; nothing was right about what was in front of him. Well, he'd take another look. Squatting down on the road, he looked back; nothing coming, the road was empty and silent. He paused, he'd surprise it!

Perhaps the squatting wasn't a great thing to have done. Fuck. His vision did a sharp 180° sweep, a wave of nausea and a sharp breath in. Shouldn't be this pissed, it was 2 am. He thought about it; squatting in the middle of a main road at 2 am was not the sharpest of moves.

No, he'd just stand up, which brought on a fresh onslaught of dizziness and nausea. But with whatever that was in the middle of the bridge, he wasn't going any further. He'd go back; where was he going back to, and to what? It was three miles back to town, it was 2 am; fuck, all was open at 2 am.

No, it was irrational, but being this drunk on a Friday night and wobbling around in the road freezing to death wasn't very fucking rational either. But what the fuck was it, and why didn't he seem to be able to walk another step closer?

The sound of a car coming in the opposite direction brought a surge of hope. The lights would illuminate it and he'd see what it was. But the car; who was in it, could it be the police? He had a bag of resin in his pocket, fuck, if it was that fucker from Bridgeton, mate, he would fuck him up just for being out and drunk. He'd hide: where? The hedge, ah yeah, that seemed like a plan.

Crawling into the hedge at the side of the road he was sure he was now invisible. The levels of shit in the hedge came as a bit of a surprise. Coke and beer bottles, a discarded pair of girls' pants, and a copy of Playboy; in his mind, and using 'drunk logic' the things all added up.

The car slowed, the exhaust had a hole in it and the farty noise it made caused him to giggle: 'farty car', hilarious. He tried to make himself smaller, but the car wasn't stopping and accelerated away in a cloud of oil smoke and farty exhaust noises.

Extricating himself from the hedge took a little more effort than he'd first imagined. Fucking brambles; he didn't want to tear his jacket, No, all good, he had mud on his knees, and there was a faint smell of piss; fuck, he thought, had he pissed himself? No, not his, someone else's, but why knickers and a copy of Playboy and the smell of piss?

Looking up, it was still there; his right eye wouldn't focus properly, and no matter how he placed his feet, he seemed to not catch his balance. But it was still there: was he scared? To be fair, he was shit scared; that just didn't look right.

The only way forward was across the bridge. He'd climb back through the hedge and cross the field, but then he had the river to cross. It was too cold and wet, and canvas shoes were not the way forward in the cold and wet grass. Fuck, it was really cold now. He buried his hands in his pockets looking for some warmth. His dad would be laughing now, taking the piss about him always being cold.

If he lit a cigarette; he'd be visible to whatever that was. Did it just move? He wasn't sure. He sat on the kerb; fuck, it was cold. Perhaps he could light the fag like his granddad had taught him, inside his coat, like in the trenches during the war. Fumbling around, he found the squashed packet of Marlboro and a BIC lighter. The effort of removing the cigarette from the packet took all his drunk brain power. Tucking his head inside his jacket, he flicked the lighter; it was one or two times before it worked.

He drew the smoke deep into his lungs, and exhaled sharply; this made him feel both dizzy and sick all at the same time, his non-focussing right eye sprang back into life, and vision seemed to briefly clarify, before sinking back into blurovision again. Could it see the glow of his cigarette? He had it cupped in his right hand, holding it between his forefinger and thumb, just like his granddad taught him. Nah, good enough to fool a German sniper, good enough to hide from that, he thought; but what the fuck was it?

2:30 am; his Hamilton watch had illuminated hands. He'd been here for thirty minutes. Whatever it was, it swayed slightly and seemed to turn and look at him. Fuck, did it take a step this way?

His arse was cold sitting on the kerb. He could just fall asleep and maybe when it was light there'd be a way to see it. His eyes were heavy, tired. Ah, yeah, tired and drunk and stoned and fucking cold! Wake up, you silly fucker, he berated himself, but no matter how cold and mashed he was, whatever that was in the road, he wasn't going past.

2:45 am; the giddy feeling returned. He'd have another fag and a think. With the anti-sniper tactic employed, he took a drag on the cigarette. It moved again; fuck, it was a murdering loony out to hack drunk teenagers to death! No, it kind of swayed again; his focus did a swoopy lunge at correcting itself and then slipped back into 'drunk mode'. No, he was going to die on the road, hacked to death by a crazed killer.

Cigarette finished, he flicked it onto the road. The cold fresh air was doing nothing for his state of drunkenness. He did, at this point, wonder: why he was that pissed? There, what was that tinkling sound? He'd heard it as if listening through a wall; there was a faint tinkle sound, like chains dragging on the road. Fuck! *The fucker had chains! I'm fucked*, he thought; whispering into the darkness, his breath made small clouds of steam.

The tinkling grew louder. *That's it, fuck, it's coming for me, but why did it seem to be in the same place, and why was it now twisting and looking directly at him? Will they find my body? Will it be quick in the end, or will I get tortured first?* All these thoughts wobbled their way through his alcohol and drug-riddled mind.

Tinkle, tinkle, and now a whine; what was it whining for? Tinkle, tinkle, whine, whir; *shit, it's a fucking alien, it's fucking hovering, that's the spaceship. I'm going to get abducted,* he thought! Whine, tinkle, whir, rumble; the new sound added to the rising fear he felt. *I mustn't piss my pants*, he thought. *I do need a piss though, and it would be warm…* Drunk logic at work again…There was a dim single light approaching along the road in the direction of the town. He felt the panic begin to rise.

That's it, he thought, *I'll jump through the hedge when the aliens get here. The fucker on the bridge called his friends; I'm sure those fuckers are coming to get me, and he has me stuck between the river and the road.*

The tinkling grew louder, the light brighter. He stood up; *I'm not dying sitting on the kerb*, he thought.

Standing unsteadily on the road, he waited for the inevitable death ray, the chains, the alien hands clasping around his neck. Shit, fuck, shit, the expletives poured out, for fuck's sake…

The light was mere feet away at this point; drunkenly wobbling, he stood his ground. *I'll die like a man; well, one that is very pissed, cold and fucking scared.*

"You alright, mate?" The voice had him recoil with shock; fucking aliens speak with a north London accent!

"You look farkin froze, mate, get in, you'll catch your farkin death of cold out here, where the fark ya goin at this time a night?"

He climbed into the glass fibre cab of the Co-op milk float; it was no fucking warmer inside the cab than out, but the seat wasn't a kerb. The 'Milky' was wrapped up in a flat cap and scarf, his fingerless mittens gripped the wheel, and his white Co-op jacket shone in the dim light of the cab.

The milk float accelerated as if a milk float could accelerate…it was more like it developed, but to his drunk mind, it was warp speed, and he couldn't understand why the world moved so fast.

They approached the bridge; the shape was still there, it twisted, turned and looked as if it jumped. He was on the edge of blind panic. The milkman was fucking fearless, surely he could see it. Perhaps they were in it together; they'd abduct him, torture him, and he'd die in a horror show of blood and gore!

The sense of panic reached a crescendo; the milk float slowed by the slight rise in the bridge, drew level with the apparition. He couldn't bring himself to look; he was scared into sobriety, and as the milk float gathered speed on the downslope of the bridge, the white plastic fertiliser bag hanging in the tree by baler twine swung around, as if in a last mocking gesture.

"Nah then, son," the milky motioned toward his bag on the seat, "flask of tea in there: wanna brew to get warm?"

Chapter 2
Warm and Fuzzy

Mid-summer evening. The bike accelerated, the crisp sound echoing back and forth off the hedgerows. Two-stroke engines love the humid summer air; the exhaust pipes crackled as he up-shifted; the bike surged forwards as the revs climbed; in his head, he was Randy Mamola; in real life, he delivered fruit and veg for a greengrocer.

It wasn't cold, which made a change; the day had been hot, thousands of thunder flies, a day that seemed to stretch to infinity. The idea for a ride out with his friend had taken but a moment.

"We should go to that pub on the Downs, wanna go?"

Swooping along the back lanes, with hedges on either side of the road now, as the speed increased, the road seemed impossibly narrow. The noise of the two bikes harmonised occasionally, and at times, the engines were out of sync as throttles and gears were not matched, the sound resonating inside his head.

But the country smells and the warm air, the buzz of the bikes made everything feel as if the world was right; and if he could only stop his left foot from hurting when he changed up through the gearbox, it would be better. The 'All-Stars' of course, perfect for riding a bike.

Rolling into the town, they were swallowed up by the lights and noise, the Saturday evening flow of folks heading out for the night.

The bike felt less alive, pottering along. This part of the town was known for its local traffic police. The merciless 'Humph', the local motorcycle cop; he'd caught his mate a few weeks before at over 100mph on the road to Bedford. The fuckers had taken his licence for a year.

The traffic lights turned red as the two bikes approached. He caught neutral, the green light in the clock winking on, he sat, arms folded, the bike ticking over unevenly beneath him. His mate looked across and nodded; they scanned for 'Humph', but he wasn't on his perch by the Co-op.

Girls roamed in packs, arm in arm, summer bought out the short skirts and skimpy tops, all flicked back hair and lots of Saturday night make-up.

He eased in the clutch, snicked the bike into first gear, the idle dipped and he caught it on the revs, the expansion chambers crackled.

The light took an age; two lads in a Mk1 Ford Escort pulled up next to the bikes. He looked across, the windows were down and a cigarette was clasped in the driver's fingers, the smoke curled up, the stereo was up loud; and as he caught the look of the two lads, the word 'wankers' was easy to lip read.

He blushed slightly. *Why the fuck am I embarrassed, what a pair of twats! All fucking disco shit and a clapped-out Escort, fuck's sake, mate*. He looked again, no 'Humph' in his spot, fucking magpie bastard, he didn't see the other fucker who was usually there with his dog van, fat pie-eating fucker, he was. Game on.

He flicked his right wrist; the bike crackled again, puffs of smoke exiting the pipes, heads turned and looked. His mate caught the idea; the two bikes now, revs rising and falling and the noise reaching out to echo off the buildings.

Green; pouring the revs on, the bike shot forwards, the front wheel skimming three or four inches off the ground, the noise reaching a cacophony of screams, second, third, fourth gear, that was at least three times the speed limit. They eased off, the Ford Escort left trailing in the wake of two-stroke smoke and failure.

As they exited the town, they turned right and back onto country lanes that led to the Downs. He'd never been to this pub, but his mate was all about it being a great spot, and normally it had 'a fair few bikes there on a Saturday night.'

The pub sat back from the road with a small parking area in front. There was no garden as such, and the few chairs outside were full; couples sat with friends, cigarettes in hand, pints of lager, and Bacardi and cokes all round, it seemed. No fucking bikes though. He really thought his mate was a dick at this point: given the level of flared trousers, and BMWs in the parking, it wasn't a place for anyone with a bike. *Ho fuckin hum*, he thought. *Ah well, we'll have a drink.*

He didn't drink and ride his bike; his reckoning was that he was a dangerous fucker as it was, no need to add alcohol to the mix. No, he'd have his usual pint of orange and lemonade: his mate looked on with disdain as he ordered, "A pint of Carlsberg, and an orange and lemonade, mate, please."

The landlord looked them up and down, grunted, poured the pint, and then fussed around mixing the two soft drinks:

"Ice?" He asked. Shaking his head, he looked away from the bar; the pub was crowded. Saturday night, summer, the smells inside a heady mix of perfume, beer, cigarettes, and what was that cheap fucking aftershave this guy is wearing...fuck me!

He took a sip of the drink, fuck, it was really sweet and sugary, but lasted longer than a coke; probably rotted the teeth more.

There was a space at a table; they headed over, crash helmet in one hand, pint in the other. He wasn't a lad who wore the normal leather jacket biker kit. Tonight, he had on a red Harrington, some jeans given to him by his boss's daughter (Levi 501s she'd bought in the US, he was dead proud) his 'go-to' reference All-Stars, a t-shirt with 'The Clash' written on it; the bike kit was Moto-x gloves, and a Nolan helmet with a dark visor, which would be a fucking nightmare for the ride home on strange roads in the dark.

He sat down, pulled a packet of cigarettes from the inside of his jacket, offered one to his mate, lit up and leant back in the chair. They got some 'looks' from the locals; they were strangers in a strange land of lots of money, farmers' daughters and 'Young Farmers' out to impress. He didn't really give a fuck. The chat went back and forth; work, work, money, the lack of money. Had he seen Kev had a new bike? The fucker always seemed to have a new bike, that, and a new car. He was a train-building apprentice; what the fuck did he do in his spare time, rob fucking banks?

The conversation ebbed and flowed, sometimes they lapsed into silence, both lost in thought; his mate was a ginger kid from the new town; he didn't even recall how they'd met; but a trip to Brighton, and getting stoned, pissed and sleeping on the pebble beach had somehow made a bond. Bikes, they did that; unlikely people who became mates, just because of two wheels, why was that?

His mate had gone onto coke, a pint was enough on the bike, and he needed his licence intact, and getting stopped on a Saturday night was more a certainty than anything.

Another cigarette. He'd taken his jacket off. The pub was hot inside, and beads of sweat broke out on his forehead; he felt sticky and out of sorts. Another ten minutes and they'd fuck off. He'd had enough of the atmosphere, and the looks from the local agriculturalists…

Looking up from the concentration needed to light yet another Marlboro, he noticed two girls sitting alone at a table. They didn't seem to fit, not wearing the go-to reference garb of the farmers' daughters. The one girl was blond, she had the brightest blue eyes; they seemed to stare right into his soul; and when she laughed at something her friend had said, her cheeks dimpled. She was very pretty. The other girl had short dark hair and a small mouth; she seemed to have a scowl; the world was not all it should be for her.

He wasn't shy and didn't need any encouragement to talk to girls. In some ways, it was like he could build characters in his head, then use the persona he'd built to go and ask a girl to dance or to just say hello.

Nobody was talking to them, none of the local 'Henrys' seemed at all interested. Were they ugly? He didn't think so; blondie had gone to the toilet and her friend was left alone twiddling the front of her blouse. Blondie walked with confidence: upright, tall, shoulders back, a posture like a dancer. She came back to the table; glancing around, she spotted the two boys at the table and for a moment their eyes met. He looked away, not wishing to seem to be staring.

His mate gave a nudge under the table, a childish grin, "You fancy some of that, eh," he looked back at him.

"Fuck off; you're such a dick sometimes."

The look was enough; he was interested. The bar was full now, the noise of conversation and the heat of the evening made the atmosphere almost stifling. He looked again; she was sitting back, relaxed, confident in her skin. The locals seemed terrified of the two girls alone at a table as if it was 'not the done thing'. He was baffled, nobody spoke to them. Maybe they were out of bounds, daughters of the local big wig farmer. who the fuck knew.

He looked at his mate. As he was ginger and it was hot, the day had been hot, and he had been outside all day, he looked red enough to spontaneously combust.

"You wanna go, mate?"

"Ah no, I'll finish my coke."

He looked at the drink; it must be warm as piss at this point. He'd had it clasped in his hand the last thirty minutes and it was warm when he got it.

"Fuck it, I'm gonna ask that girl if she wants a drink."

His friend looked at him like he'd got two heads! "You farkin mad, mate, she's someone's Doris mate, you'll get a slap."

"No, nobody has been near her all night mate and we've been here in this fuckin boring as fuck pub for an hour and a half. It closes in thirty minutes, and I'm bored beyond fucking belief, and she's really good-looking, nice legs."

He stood up and reached in his pocket for the last five quid he had with him; he'd scrape home on the petrol that he had.

He picked up Ginger's glass, "Want another?"

"Ah fuck no, fucking boring."

The girl looked up; he moved through the crowd and as he pushed through a couple of locals, he approached the table. Time seemed to stand still; the pub went very quiet. No, he imagined it; he placed the glass on the bar, turned and looked at the girl. She smiled.

"Can I buy you a drink?" Her smile widened. Then a great roar of applause and wolf whistles filled the pub!

He looked around. The local 'Henrys' were in raptures, clapping and whistling, looking at him and laughing. He stepped back, hackles raised at this point.

One of the locals stepped out from the throng, "That's for you! The applause I mean. We all had bets who would be first, and you won! Oh, so much fun."

He looked back and just nodded. "Fuck me, you guys are short of shit to do mate, eh?" His London accent came to the fore when he was a bit riled up. The local took offence, looking across at his friends for moral support. They looked down into their pints; seemingly, 'Henry' was on his own.

The girl mouthed 'sorry' and smiled.

"What did you want?" He asked.

The cacophony of sound had died away, the locals' thirty-second point of interest gone; they were probably back to talking about tractors or combines or some such shit.

"Gin and tonic, please."

"And your mate?"

He winced inside as the cost of a G&T plus another drink would have him borrowing money off Ginger.

"She's fine."

He breathed out and waved the fiver at the landlord. "G&T, mate, please."

The landlord nodded, grinned like a loon, and pushed a glass into the optic for a measure of gin.

The evening hadn't really cooled down, the summer had been warm. They pushed the bikes and walked the two girls the short distance to the house where the dark-haired girl lived. Blondie was an actress and a singer, staying in the country with her friend, you know, West End stage and shows. Had he ever been? No, he'd not been to any West End shows; he'd seen the Stranglers in Brixton Academy the other week though; did she know them? She looked puzzled; Stranglers? Her incredible blue eyes grew wider when she said it.

Chapter 3
The Smoke

"No, it's fine, it's just I'm running out of ten-pence coins, yes, Saturday? Yes, that's great, no, I'll have to get the train, what? No, the train, to Euston right?"

She answered in the affirmative. Beep, beep, beep: the phone was demanding more ten-pence coins. The phone box stank of the regulation piss, and he was holding the handset using his sleeve; he'd wiped the mouthpiece with the same sleeve, better remember to not put that anywhere near his mouth.

"Yes, can you meet me, what? No, I'll see what time the train gets in," beep, beep, beep, "Sorry, I don't have any more change, oh wait, two pence! Hang on, yes, I'll call you." Click, burr, the phone went dead.

He'd have to suffer the ritual humiliation of asking his mum if he could use the phone; it was locked up with a rotary dial lock. I mean, who the fuck puts on a rotary dial lock? He could always undo it; he knew where she put the key; or if he popped out the middle of the dial, he could remove it and dial the number with a pair of pliers. Either way, he'd call the blonde girl and set the time to meet the train.

The station waiting room was full, so he stood outside on the platform. The morning was chill, and he'd regretted not taking a jacket. He'd swapped his go-to red Harrington for a blue and black 1950s bowling shirt: the name above the left breast pocket read 'Rick', and the logo on the rear advertised 'Ricks Auto-shop Monterey California'. The 501s were still in attendance, but he'd found a pair of skater shoes in a really cool store in Northampton. The logo read 'Vans'; he'd never heard of them, but they looked cool: black suede, with a white band around the sole, and they'd cost the best part of a week's wages. Who the fuck is Van anyway? They went with the outfit, and the 501s were turned up at the bottom with two turns on the end…His boss' daughter had really long legs!

The train clunked and clanked its way into the station, doors opened, folks climbing aboard, the heavy doors slammed shut, some fitting better than others. He reminded himself that half the guys he knew built the carriages: he really must get a car!

The carriage smelled of stale tobacco, mould, and that odd smell of dust that the horrible patterned British Rail seats always smelled of. The last time he'd caught a train was a few weeks before. He'd gone with his brother to Whitechapel Hospital to see a specialist, then he'd felt pretty shit as his brother was admitted to the hospital as the infection in his bones was out of control. Fuck's sake, he'd been there three weeks, and was coughing up yellow gunk, he swore it was the London air.

He looked through the grime-covered window: the countryside rolled past, the images flickering as if it was a cartoon. He'd not thought much about taking the trip to see the girl. She'd called him one evening; he was a little surprised.

They'd swapped numbers, and there had been the briefest of kisses: he'd held her face in his hands when they kissed. He saw it in a film once, and it seemed to be the thing to do. She had the brightest blue eyes, almost the first thing he'd seen that night in the pub on the Downs.

They'd chatted on the phone. Her accent had no London twang to it, far from it; she sounded kind of posh, money; he'd noticed the first night they'd met. He really felt a bit out of sorts speaking to her. Depending on the amount of time he spent with his dad, depended on how 'London' his accent was. His dad would drop deep into his cockney accent when he'd been into London with the lorry, and he'd noticed that he rolled into the same accent, like a mimic. He was good at that though.

The train clattered and rattled its way towards London. The scene changed to the suburban sprawl and then, as they got deeper into the city, he noticed the backs of the houses, how folks would dump grass cuttings and garden waste over a wall into the side of the line. Rolling into the city, the carriages rattled over the points, visibly shaking they twisted and turned on the bogies beneath. Coming into a city on the train laid bare all the grime and dirt, no frontages, just the harsh rear views of shops, factories and houses. Imagine living amongst this, he thought: why the fuck would you want to?

Euston was an assault on the senses after his regional station; noisy tinny announcements, the throng of humanity dashing forwards, all in a rush to get to wherever and to whatever they were doing; they seemed in a hurry to do it.

She'd wait at the platform. He'd told her which train, and although he wasn't sure about the time it took to get there, he really hoped she wouldn't stand him up. The humanity thinned a little, and there at the end of the platform stood a blonde girl in a flowery summer dress, her blond hair pulled back into a ponytail, her eyes darting from person to person, searching for his face, or the red jacket. She wasn't sure he'd come; but looking through the crowd, she saw him, the flat-top hair and the shirt had him standing out from the crowd.

Their eyes met, and she smiled: her eyes did the soul-boring exercise. He blushed, what the fuck for? He'd no idea. She did look very pretty though.

"You came," the words smiled their way out of her mouth.

He looked at her for a moment, unsure of where to put his feet; his hands were clammy and he felt 'difficult' out of any kind of comfort zone. Had they even been invented yet?

"Hello."

The word sounded as difficult as it had been to say, his confidence evaporated along with the people on the platform.

Her turn to look a little awkward. "I have a day planned for us; what time is your train back?"

Fuck me, he'd only just arrived and she had him on the train home!

"I didn't get a return, I thought we'd see how the time is, and I'll get a ticket later."

She did that smile thing again, and the eyes took another lap around his soul; fuck me, it's unnerving when she does that.

She took his hand. Her hand was small, the skin pale, and there was no sign of the summer on her skin at all. She had the look of someone who spent time in the shade: was she a vampire? He'd soon find out.

They walked into the sunshine outside the station, and she confidently hailed a black cab. "Kensington Gore please." The cabby nodded.

She sat back, legs crossed; she had on a pair of black Dr Martin shoes, and small white socks; a world of confidence flowed from her.

"I have to call and see my friend Rachel. She has a script for me, will only take a moment."

He nodded, the world spun briefly; he'd got Kensington and Rachel, a script. Who the fuck was this girl?

Rachel was not what he'd expected: short, with a mass of curly out-of-control hair; she'd bubbled with enthusiasm when they met. The girl dropped the script into her bag, gave Rachel a peck of a kiss on the cheek, and they walked away.

"Are you hungry?" She asked.

He nodded, "Starving."

"Oh, dear, we'll have to do something about that."

They crossed the main road, headed into Kensington Gardens, up towards Kensington House. Perhaps she had relations there? Who's to know?

"What would you like?"

"I'd love a cuppa tea and a bacon sandwich, mate."

He caught himself. 'Mate'. Didn't sound like he should call her mate. No, that wouldn't do, would it? She smiled again and the eyes did another lap. Shit, he'd not expected her openness, and the smile was the most disarming thing he'd ever seen. She took his hand again and he relaxed into the moment, releasing some of the tightness he had. She matched his stride; her upright posture made him feel like an ape, and he made an effort to walk taller and lift his head.

They'd crossed the park; he hadn't really noticed. They'd chatted. He found he didn't need to make an effort; she spun words out, projecting and annunciating the sounds, her voice had an almost musical lilt to it. Good job really; she did say she was a singer.

They sat outside a cafe on the edge of the park. She ordered Earl Grey. He'd had that once at his friend's house in the village, he thought it tasted like soap. His mate's mum had laughed like a drain, but it was ten thirty in the morning, and she was usually pissed by nine-thirty, and she'd laugh at anything. He had a cup of 'builder's' and two sugars, a bacon sandwich.

"Can you cut the rind off love, please?" Ketchup and he wolfed the sandwich down as if the world would end, and it was his last meal.

"Where to?" He asked.

"Well, the Victoria and Albert Museum. Have you been?"

No, he'd not been. It wasn't far. They passed the Albert Hall; amazing really how much of London was dedicated to a bloody German: hadn't they been to war twice and only won the World Cup once?

The museum passed in a blur of facts and history. She wanted to take him to Soho, Piccadilly Circus and Leicester Square. Fine by him, he was a tourist for the day; the last time he'd seen this much of London was when he got lost finding fucking Brixton. It was warm, the late summer heat bounced back from the pavement. They strolled. It seemed a posher way of walking than just walking. He hadn't done much strolling before.

Was it dinner time yet? She smiled; she looked at him with curious eyes. "Dinner?"

Yeah. He glanced at the faithful Hamilton. "It's half twelve, I'm getting hungry again." He had the metabolism of a rat: could eat endlessly and never seemed to be full, well, unless it was one of his dad's Sunday roasts, then he'd be full to bursting.

"Ah, lunchtime," she said. The eyes did another lap. He felt she really did have a window into his thoughts. Good job he'd painted over them before he left.

"Would you like a steak?" Steak, ah yeah; he recalled an embarrassing incident with a Royal Marines recruit sergeant. He'd fancied being a Marine, and when they had had a careers day at school (he'd been there that day, he didn't know why, he'd picked up the leaflet at the table). The Marine had looked at him. He was dressed in a green shirt and had his beret razor-sharp with the globe and anchor over his eye.

"Alright son?" He'd asked.

He looked back at the Marine; he was a fucking building not a bloke, his moustache trimmed to perfection.

"Fancy some of that life, do ya son?"

He'd looked at the brochure: a Marine was poised to leap ashore from a rubber boat.

"Well, dunno, mate," he saw the sergeant wince at the word 'mate'.

"Well, son, it's hard but the benefits are great: travel, action, and all the steak you can eat."

"Steak?" He'd asked.

The sergeant looked him square in the eye, his lip twitched slightly.

"Yeah, if you want two or three, you can have 'em; full English every day, build you up, like."

He'd looked back at the Marine, glancing down at the table. He saw an FN rifle, no magazine in it. It looked black and kind of mean, not like the plastic one he'd bought in Woolworths as a kid that ejected plastic bullets.

"Do I get one of those?"

"Yes, my son, once you've earned, like." The sergeant looked at him again: "What's up son?" He asked.

He'd looked back: "Sorry mate, but what's a steak?"

The sergeant's eyes lit up. "Wanna sign here son? We'll have you down for a tryout, see if you like it!"

Meanwhile, back in London, they'd made their way to a grill off Leicester Square; the waiter fussed them to a table for two near a window. Called him 'sir' and her madam. Fuck's sake mate, a bit over the top.

She did that confidence thing again, nothing unsettled her. She'd asked for water. "Yes, ice please." He'd never had water with ice, he felt very fucking rural at this point. She reached across the table, took both his hands and did the disarming smile thing again. "Are you always this on edge?" It was a question; eh was he? He'd never noticed.

"I'm okay." He lied so convincingly.

The waiter arrived again, could he take the order? She would have a cheeseburger, medium, hold the onions, and can she have fries on the side? The waiter nodded his approval. And for sir? Man, that made him itch; he worked for a living and was on the same level as the lad asking the question. "Ah, can I have the same please?" Chickens way out, but when in doubt, mimic. And to drink, she'd have a glass of red wine; no it didn't matter, house was fine. And for sir?

He winced again, "Can I get a Guinness, mate, please?" 'Mate' again, he had to stop.

The burgers and drinks arrived; the waiter fussed around placing the plates, and asking again if all was okay. It was, thanks. She noticed he never spoke when he was eating, his entire concentration focussed on the food, she thought for a moment she'd done something wrong…but no, the act of eating was absolute, and once he'd cleaned his plate and split the G on his Guinness, he looked up, his brown eyes lit up and smiling at her, he launched into telling her about wanting to see a band called Bauhaus, she thought it was an art school in Germany…

Food dispensed with, they headed back to Leicester Square; the Odean cinema was showing 'Fame'. Had he seen it? Um, no, he'd not seen it, it wasn't high on his list of films to see. The last film he'd seen was Airplane, and he'd actually cried laughing. They 50/50'd the tickets, like the lunch; everything was squared away. She insisted, and he'd carried along with the ride. It was fine, he was blowing a month of savings on a day with a girl he hardly knew, in a city he barely knew, watching a film he'd never ordinarily watch. They snuggled into the seats. Her eyes were wide, they'd probably melt the fucking screen. The theme tune carried away into the end credits, what next?

A pub for a drink? They'd ended up by the Thames. Wandering past the Houses of Parliament, they ended up outside Westminster Abbey. *We should go inside.* Ah, yeah, he'd seen that Kipling was buried there. Didn't he make cakes? She looked at him with a blank expression, cakes, she asked. He was laughing at his own joke, and finally she caught on, and giggled, cakes…

They wandered along until they were outside a place called the 'Westminster arms'. We'll have a drink. He looked inside; there were quite a few pairs of Dr Martins boots, short jeans above the boots and black Harrington jackets. A pub full of skinheads!

"You sure?" He asked, "Not sure I'm okay in there."

She looked puzzled; his whole Rockabilly outfit was lost on her. She hadn't a clue that the flat-top hair and the shirt etc. would see him beaten to a pulp in the alley next to the pub.

"It's fine," she chirped. "There were some seats on the pavement," he'd sit his arse down there and let her deal with the ordering.

"Oi Rockabilly!" The voice was deep and guttural. He took a moment to un-shit his pants. Four lads sat at a table just inside the door. He tried not to look.

"Fuck me, mate, you're a brave lad, aintcha?"

He looked down, not wishing the confrontation.

She was chirping away at the barman. "Yes, a Guinness and a G&T please."

The skinheads laughed. He looked up and met the big lad's eyes straight on. The lad nodded, saw the lack of intent, and nodded again at his mates. No words were needed, back to their pints and no doubt conversations about the National Front and killing black folks at Notting Hill carnival.

They sat in the sunshine, an odd silence consumed him. He felt out of place but of the place. He'd tell her of his dad and his cousin Julia, who sang with the big swing band during the war; how his dad was raised like a 'show brat' for a time, getting dragged around the West End from party to party; 'have a lemonade lad, no, she's busy.'

They wandered down the embankment, reaching Cleopatra's Needle. The Sphynx beneath made a spot to stop and take in the Thames rolling swiftly by. His nan's folks had been 'wherrymen', did she know the term? She shook her head. He explained the French heritage, and how they worked the river and the estuary. "How fascinating." It was, eh? He hadn't thought about it much, but I guess the river was home in a way.

They sat on the steps by the Sphynx; it seemed appropriate to kiss the girl. Her skin glowed in the early evening light, and he felt as if they'd known each other for more than just the day. Soppy wanker, what the fuck: it was just a Doris. For sure, she was pretty, very, as it happened, great legs and the posture put him to shame. Anyway; he kissed her again and she kissed him back. The Sphynx didn't bat an eyelid; they'd seen it all before.

Chapter 4
Stage Fright

Could he come to town again? It was almost a month since he'd seen her, his new job had kept him busy with overtime, and he'd not been able to get away. The phone line crackled an audible hiss. What was that? He'd had such a great time with her before, and didn't want for it to become 'complicated'. The last girl he'd been seeing had dumped him for his mate's brother, who in turn found out that she wasn't his type. He'd wanted to shag her in the back of the car, and she wasn't 'that kind of girl', thanks very much. So he'd left her in the rain outside the Chinese restaurant in Bridgeton, kind of served her right in a way. He'd not been able to compete with the Ford Capri, and his sharp suits anyway. The grass is always greener 'an all that'.

The last time he saw her, they'd had a great day, and the train ride home had been a bit flat and sad. She'd had to go as her friends were waiting for her for a birthday party. She never said whose, but he got that it was not to be missed. She'd gone with him to the station, and he'd bought the ticket back with almost the last of his cash. He'd have to call his mate for a lift home from the station.

She'd looked deep into his eyes. He really wanted to look away, but somehow he was transfixed by her. He'd muttered something about her being very beautiful. She'd blushed, her skin glowed from the day of walking (or did they stroll now?), her clear blue eyes did another loop around his soul, and she'd kissed him again. She turned away. He swore that she floated across the floor of the station as she hurried away towards the underground. It was at that point he realised he didn't even know her last name.

Yes, he could come, but he had to go to Whitechapel Hospital to see his brother. He was still in the hospital. Yes, he was alone in a single room.

"Oh, poor lamb!"

He laughed at that and couldn't wait to tell his brother that he was a 'poor lamb'; but his brother was connected to various pipes and tubes. The infection in his bones had got no better and they were trying vast amounts of different antibiotics, and a thing he thought he was sure they called a 'pipe drain'. Either way, it looked fucking horrible: a tube ran from his side into a glass jar beneath the bed his brother was in. He spent the whole time just staring out the window and reading bike magazines. His dad called down to see him as often as he could. He was into London a lot with loads of bricks, and found he could leave the trailer at his old army mucker's builder's yard, and run up with the tractor unit to the hospital; it wasn't far from the Commercial Rd.

He'd called her again. A man's voice answered the phone. "Oh, darling, it's for you, yes, I think it's that boy again."

Boy? Fuck me, mate, boy…

"Hello?" There she was again, the accent and the manner.

"Listen, I have to go see my brother. Can you meet me at the hospital, or is that too far out of your way?"

"No, it's fine."

They agreed the time, and he told her to come up to the ward. The Irish sister in charge of the wards was fearsome, scared the shit out of him; but she'd taken a shine to his brother, and he could get away with almost anything, including visitors at odd hours.

Would he like to come to the theatre? She was rehearsing for a musical, and they would need to go after seeing his brother.

"Yes, sounds great!" He actually had no idea what it sounded like. Theatre?

His brother looked pale and ill when he got there, mainly because he was. The lack of sunlight on his normally dark skin left him looking waxy, and his skin looked almost see-through and shone with that shine that sick people seemed to have. He'd bought him three packets of B&H cigarettes. No, they didn't have number 6's, he'd have to suffer those. In the Co-op carrier bag, he'd added some grapes, a bottle of orange squash, two Mars bars, and a copy of 'Bike Magazine'.

She'd found the ward. He'd seen her walking up the corridor, her now unmistakable stance; her hair was shorter than before, much shorter; she looked almost elfin-like. The eyes shone when she saw him, she made a waving motion with her left hand. She had on a pair of jeans, suede boots, and a short grey jacket over a blouse. He'd not noticed the Star of David necklace the last time they'd met, perhaps it was new.

He stood, took two steps forward and met her at the door. Her eyes did the usual deep dive into his consciousness and he felt a wave of warmth spread up through his face. Her smile brightened the room. His brother had remained quiet during their embrace, and then he'd cracked a smile and reached out to take her hand. "Hello, I'm Nick."

She'd reached forward and kissed him on both cheeks. "Hi Nick," she glanced around the room. "It's a bit austere, isn't it?"

Nick smiled. "Ah yeah, just a bit. I get a view though. I get to watch the pigeons shagging on the roof."

She chuckled, smiling. "How long do you expect to stay, Nick?" She asked.

"I'm not sure, another couple of weeks I think, they tell me the drugs are working, I can't wait to get home, I'm bored, and London is really noisy."

She nodded, small talk flowed back and forth, and then she glanced at her watch:

"Do we have to go?" He asked.

"We do, rather," she said. There it was again; the accent and the way she used the words in all the correct order. Amazing.

From the entrance of the hospital, she'd waved to a black cab. She leaned into the window. "Aldwych Theatre, please."

The cabby did that thing that they do, nodding and flicking the meter on. He sat back and watched as the cabby plied his trade, weaving through the traffic, the odd curse here and there. The cabby glanced back in his mirror, taking in the lad sitting with the pretty blonde girl.

He'd had a bit of a change of look. The autumn was fast approaching and the days not so warm; damp and chill in fact. On his last visit to his granddad, he'd 'borrowed' one of his flat caps; it was light brown colour, no pattern as such; he had it pushed back on his head, with the front of the 'flat-top' haircut sticking out at the front. He'd found some vintage jeans in the shop in Northampton, and he'd turned them up two or three times. A red check shirt was buttoned all the way up, and a pair of Clarks 'desert welly' suede boots. To top off that look, he'd found a Herringbone pattern overcoat in Help the Aged, for two quid; he was essentially dressed like his granddad.

He watched London pass by, the condensation building on the inside of the cab window; he wiped it away with his sleeve, which just made it smear and more difficult to see out of. Her hand had unconsciously found his, and she intertwined her fingers with his. She was looking out the other window, lost in thought. They didn't need to seem to say much, comfortable in each other's company.

"I'll drop you off here, love," the cabby motioned towards the front of the theatre.

"Thanks, very kind," she reached into her bag to pay. The cabby's thick fingers reached back through the window. He nodded, took the change, flicked the meter, and they stepped out onto the street. The weather was doing that mizzle kind of drizzle thing. She took his arm in hers, and they stepped through the wood and glass doors into the theatre.

It all felt a bit odd. He really felt out of place, the surroundings were not his, and the lobby was full of hustle and bustle of busy-looking people.

"Darling, there you are," the guy wooshed across the lobby, taking both her hands in his and kissing her on both cheeks. "I'm so glad you're here. We can get started."

She motioned to introduce the boy, but the other guy had turned away and was dashing across the lobby to open a door towards the interior of the theatre and, disappointed by his lack of interest, she followed. He felt invisible.

At this point, he was having doubts about being there; his self-confidence was having a meeting with his nervous system, and they'd both decided that here was not probably where they needed to be. If he could only stop blushing and clinging to her hand like a child, he may feel better; but here he was having a major crisis, and for fucks sake, who was this girl? Everyone seemed to greet her like a star; for him, she was the girl from the Downs and a kiss by the lions at Cleopatra's Needle. He'd have to work this shit out, co's whatever was happening here, he felt very out of his fucking depth.

"I'll park you here," she motioned towards a seat at the side of the stage, "I must change and the others are waiting." He got odd looks from the theatre folks as they passed by. Various stagehands busied themselves with robes, lighting, and what looked like sandbags. He was dying for a cigarette at this point. But since he'd seen her the last time, he'd stopped. He looked down at his fingers: they seemed to miss the paper tube full of carcinogenic tobacco and chemicals. A bit of gum would do. He hadn't eaten for at least an hour, and he was hungry, how long did this rehearsing thing go on for? Alone, in the darkness at the side of the stage, he felt less conscious. He'd taken off the granddad coat, draped it over his lap and leant back onto the wall.

The next time he saw her, she was coming into centre stage. Other members of the cast gathered around and lots of animated conversation took place. A lad in jeans and a white t-shirt walked out. The cast seemed to part as he arrived. She turned, they looked at each other, and then from the massive speakers in the roof, the music started. He knew the tune, it was from West Side Story. He expected she was in the chorus, but no, there she was centre stage; she was the lead. Who was she? His ignorance was embarrassing. At this point, he'd melted into the chair, her voice carried high into the roof of the building, clear, and powerful. He was spellbound.

He seemed to drift through time, watching the stop and start of the rehearsal. She'd occasionally glanced his way, mouthed 'okay' and rolled back into character. Other actors nodded and smiled at him as they passed on the way to and from the dressing room. Was he okay? He wasn't sure. Mostly, he was a little lost. He'd not expected her to be the lead actress, but then he had no expectations; they were the same age. 18 seemed to be very young to be such a big West End star, but her voice and her ability to dominate the stage were evident. He'd just never expected her to be so amazing. But then, what did he expect? No fucking clue, mate, but this was surreal. It was his favourite new word, one that he seemed to be using a lot.

He'd wandered off into a little moment of his own, and there she was at his side. She looked at him, he was lost, deep in thought.

"Hey, there you are. Where do you go off to when you do that?"

He wasn't sure what 'that' was, but he was back in the room and a bit lost for words, which didn't happen very often according to his dad.

The white t-shirt guy stopped, "Hey, we're going to dinner and the club in Chelsea after, you want to come?"

She didn't know, did he want to go? To be fair, he wanted to sit down, have a pint and a fag and wonder where the world was going. He seemed to be clinging to the outside looking in and wondering where to get off. "Sure, they could go."

Dinner was in a noisy Italian restaurant. The menu seemed to be all in Italian; he wasn't sure what to order. She would have a Bruschetta and then a Carbonara; he did the mimic thing and ordered the same. The comfort zone waved hello from the other side of the room where he felt it belonged. She ordered bottles of San Pellegrino. Some of the other cast were wrapped up in animated conversations; they were incredibly loud, all hands and big teeth smiles.

Wine? The question stabbed at him. He was more a pint of Guinness, but yeah, wine would be fine…fuck, he was talking in rhymes! So embarrassing. The remaining part of his confidence left by the front door waved briefly and left for the evening.

She was attentive, she didn't leave him alone with the cast. Even when they all talked 'shop', she managed to pull him into the conversation. It turned to music, was he interested at all?

Yes, what kind? Oh, all sorts really, Bowie at the moment, but he'd been bought up on old-school rock and roll. His mum and dad would occasionally jive around the living room, much to the embarrassment of the kids.

Who was he listening to at the moment? "Well, nobody, mate, I'm here with you and I can't hear a fucking thing co's you lot are really loud; and if I could just turn the volume down a bit, I'd be able to hear, to catch a word and chime in." He was jokingly taking the piss; he wasn't sure they got it…

They looked: apparently sarcasm wasn't big in this part of town. The t-shirt guy laughed. "That's hilarious: 'turn the volume down'. Did you all hear that, we have a new stage play name!"

The food arrived. He had no idea what a Carbonara was, but the toast that came before was okay, and he washed it all down with a few glasses of white wine. A mild glow set in, the alcohol eased his tension. The self-confidence knocked at the door; he'd opened it, let it in, it sat on a stool looking uncomfortable, but it was back; and there was a chair over there, with a pint of brown and bitter, next to it, it may just get comfortable. She'd had a few glasses of wine. The place was warm, and she had that glow again he'd seen at the station. Dessert? He wasn't sure. She cast an eye down the menu: oh, Tiramisu, perfect. Would he like to try?

He was trying in the meantime to work out how much all this cost, but the production manager had the bill in his hand. "All chargeable," he'd said with a larger-than-real smile.

He caught her hand as they left the restaurant. A wave of concern had crossed his face.

"Look, I'm not sure how to get home if we go to the club. It'll be late and the last train is half eleven."

She'd looked back into his eyes again. She noticed that he had green flecks in the brown, and somehow the light outside in the street made them stand out.

"You don't need to go home, do you?" She asked. "Tomorrow is Sunday; you're not working, are you?"

He shook his head. Naively, he asked where he was going to sleep. The answer was implied, more than answered, and his self-confidence barged things aside in its rush to get back in.

It was early for the club. They'd get a few drinks in the pub first. He quite liked these theatre folks; they could certainly drink which suited him. They ended up in a pub called 'The Bunch of Grapes' off Brompton Road. The Saturday evening crowd was two deep at the bar, and they'd wedged themselves into seats in a corner. Drinks ordered, he'd noticed the number of theatre folks had dwindled. There was just the t-shirt guy—what was his fucking name? No, he couldn't remember and it was too late to ask—and the curly-haired girl he'd met before, Rachel.

Conversation rolled. They talked about London, expenses, and how they were excited about the run of the show. Rachel was into her third pint of Stella; for a little thing, she could put pints away like a builder!

"What is it you do?" The question leapt at him from the corner of Rachel's mouth.

"Err, I'm well, I um…" At this point, his self-confidence left the comfy chair and sat on a railway line; it seemed to be waiting for the '125 Special' heading for failure.

"I'm a driver." He'd try to be unspecific, but Rachel wasn't letting it go.

"Oh, yeah." Her accent was slipping, and did he detect a Norfolk twang in there?

"Yeah."

Ah fuck, it didn't matter; she knew what he did, we can't all be show stars, and he felt a bit ordinary in their company anyway.

"He drives a huge yellow dump truck." She'd jumped in to save him. He looked across, and the blue eyes twinkled back. She laughed and it was infectious; the others at the table joined in, the self-confidence sat up, pinged the railway line, listened for the oncoming train and waited patiently.

It needn't have bothered. He explained that the economic period was a bit difficult, he'd been made redundant on two occasions now, and his last job folded and left him needing the next thing that came along. Luckily, they were building a big road extension next to his mum and dad's place, and they always seemed to have a few of the Irish lads who worked the big motor scrapers leaning over the fence chatting to his dad, and drinking tea. They talked about the old country and the troubles.

When one of the foremen found out he was out of work, he asked if he could drive a tractor.

"Of course, mate."

"Well then, you can drive that." He pointed over his shoulder to a big yellow six-wheel-drive dump truck. Through the mud, he could make out the word Volvo. Twenty minutes later, he was proficient in its semi-auto gearbox, air seat and the radio worked; plus he was paid four times more than the last job. So, that's what he 'did'. He left an edge to the word, just to see if it needed to cut. As it happened, it didn't need to; seemed the theatre folk knew a thing or two about being out of work.

The itch to have a fag was turning into a raging rash now. His fingers felt unemployed, and the craving for nicotine to go with the beer was almost unbearable. But she didn't smoke, and the last thing he wanted to do was go breathing cigarette smoke in her face. She'd snugged in a little closer. She felt he needed a little close contact, and she'd put her hand on the inside of his leg. It hadn't gone unnoticed, and now his comfort zone was back looking at him in a quizzical manner. He'd get another round in. "Same again?" No, the t-shirt guy was done, and Rachel just looked pissed as a fart. She lolled into the t-shirt guy and he shrugged. "I think she needs to get home; me too. I think I'll head off, and take her with me along the way."

"Ah, okay, mate, no worries. Shall we come with you?"

"No, it's fine. I'm tired after today, the club seemed such a good idea, but I'd fall asleep in a trice." Who the fuck used words like 'trice'? He wasn't sure. As they headed for the door, Rachel wobbled a little. The earlier drizzle had done nothing for the mass of curls, they seemed to have exploded, and she had on a white roll-neck sweater. As she headed for the door, he thought she looked like a Dandelion clock!

Looking back across the bar towards where she sat, he felt something melt inside. It wasn't a comfortable melt. He was falling for this girl, and she shone; her persona stood out in a room full of people, almost as if there was another worldly aura around her. Fuck me, he had to get a grip.

He turned back to the bar, "Guinness and a G&T, please."

The girl behind the bar clocked his hat and the hair. "Nice look, mate." He blushed. *Fuck me, these girls in London, very fuckin direct.* He'd have to work on this 'blushing shy country boy thing;' it was getting on his tits.

"I didn't realise you were the lead." She looked up and sipped her drink, and the smile was back in her eyes. He still hadn't got used to them doing laps of his soul, and the more she did it, the more he thought she could read what was written inside. He'd written it backwards on a mirror, so hopefully, by the time she got all 'Bletchley Park' to work out what it said, they'd be more comfortable.

She kissed him. It was passionate, and he'd not expected it. His comfort zone dialled 999 and waited for a response. "Shall we go?"

He looked behind to find her coat, and he wanted to do that 'gentleman thing' and help her on with it. She stood up. He pulled her coat from the back of the chair and held it up for her to slip in her arms. She went to flick-back hair that was no longer there. He laughed; his eyes crinkled in the corners. He gave her a nudge, taking the piss, making silly faces.

The eyes narrowed; the lips pursed a little. "Are you mocking me?" She hissed.

Fuck, shit, fuck, was she serious, had he crossed a line? She couldn't hold the look any longer and burst out laughing. "Your face," she said, "let's head home."

999 had been answered at this point and the operator was asking, "Which emergency service?" His comfort zone was confused. They could walk from here; it wasn't far. The crowd in the pub was packed pretty tight, and they squeezed their way towards the door. He led, holding onto her hand as they motioned through the people. He looked back over his left shoulder to check she was okay, "Scuse'me, sorry, scuse me…"

There was a huge sucking sound. The air seemed to be pulled back; the glass in the doors and windows erupted into a million shards. He felt the air pulled from his lungs and the weight of the people as they were hurled against him. He lost the grip on her hand. He had no control over the forces moving him around. He tried to look back for her. She was less than a foot away, but she'd vanished into a wall of dust, glass and bodies. The blackness was all-enveloping. He felt nothing, but he could taste blood in his mouth, and he was, in his mind's eye, flailing to stand up. He swam upwards towards consciousness. The animal-like screams he heard could not be people, the dust and glass in his eyes. He called for her, but the noise he made didn't appear to be human. His consciousness left the building. He swam back to the darkness, but as he faded, he thought he heard her voice.

Chapter 5
Clear

She'd heard the same noise, almost as if time froze, the air evaporating from her lungs, and the sucking woosh sound. His fingers had been torn away. In an instant, she was lifted up, and she felt the world rotate. She looked for him, but the bodies, the dust, glass and the chaos consumed everything.

She couldn't hear. Her screams were muffled by the weight of the two men that had landed on her. The pain in her legs and the inability to breathe caused her to panic. She tried to scream, but the weight prevented her from breathing in. In an instant, the world had boiled, and her shocked numbed brain couldn't conceive what was happening. His hand was no longer there. He'd been there an instant ago, smiling and easing through the throng of people. If only she could move her legs; if only she could move. The panic boiled over, her limited breathing was out of control, and she was hyperventilating into unconsciousness.

He could hear noises, as if the sound travelled through a tunnel, and seemed to reach down to him. His subconscious brain told him to wake up. Why couldn't he hear, why couldn't he see anything? The swooping swimming sense of fighting to the surface of a dark ocean of blackness had him reaching out into the void. His right hand searched the air above himself, and he could feel the sticky slippery liquid that seemed to cover his face and his chest.

He lapsed back into the void. The swimmy feeling came and went, and he was powerless to move. Unconscious and conscious were locked in combat over the control of his senses, and they were each determined to win. As the sounds rebounded back and forth, he felt some sense of feeling returning. He couldn't move his left arm; he flailed around again with his right. The guttural sounds, almost animal-like, surrounded him now. He had the sense of hands reaching down, echoes of sound came and went; the pain in his head was unreal. Why was he wet, had he passed out and pissed himself? Unconscious seemed to win at that point.

He stepped out, briefly, and for the smallest moment in time, he looked down. It seemed he was looking at the scene of destruction from the top left-hand corner of what had once been the bar. He saw himself, could that be him? He looked a bit fucked: his left arm was under a large section of what had been the bar, and he seemed to be covered in blood. Who the fuck were those people, and why were they in different places at the same time? Body parts, blood, and who knows what the fuck that was that seemed to be sprayed up the walls.

He looked for her. She had to be there. If he could just see her, he'd know that he could leave, and as long as she was alive it wouldn't matter, he could go. He could see a girl under two men who'd fallen across her, one obviously dead, as the section of the door that was sticking out of his head certainly didn't belong there. The other guy was convulsing. Then he saw the short blond hair; her head was behind the guy's legs.

She seemed to be twitching, small shuddering pulses of movement from her arms and legs. He was powerless. He had to get back, he had to want to get back into whatever that was on the floor and live.

Shapes were above her now; she felt the weight lifted and strong hands reached down.

"Come on, Miss, we've got you. Come on, you're okay now, we'll sit you up. Can you breathe now?"

The police officer looked down at her. She was relatively unhurt; her left ear drum had been burst, and the blood trickled down her neck. She was white with dust, and the tears of panic rolled through the dust to make small tracks down her face. She was crying. An officer was trying to pick her up, but she was powerless to stand. The tears came again; the fresh wave of emotion rolled up her chest and she cried out. The scene before her rolled to the left, and she felt herself spiral into a void. She was looking up from the bottom of a well, as if a telescope had been turned around. She felt herself being covered, a red blanket pulled up, and she seemed to float out into the cold night air.

The last thing she could visualise before she faded back into the dark, was the strip light in the back of the Ford Transit ambulance.

He'd stayed in the top left-hand corner of the shattered bar and watched them clear the bodies away from her. The young officer was visibly shaking, and he was trying to get her to sit up. She swayed and he saw her cry out. It was soundless, and the pain of her cry sent shock waves through him. She was crying, her eyes wide with pain. There was blood on her face and neck, and the tears rolled down her cheeks. He wanted, at that point, to be alive. He wanted, at that point, to be there, and to be able to look into the blue in blue eyes, have her do laps around his soul. He'd show her anything she wanted to see. Her soundless cry sent shock waves of pain down his arms and into his chest. "Clear," and again, "Clear!"

There was movement. He felt hands feeling for his pulse. The sensation was even in these extreme circumstances weird. He'd felt some odd weird shit, but even an acid trip on a two-tab had nothing on this shit. He wanted to make a sound and let the hands know he was alive. Was he alive? He didn't recall. Didn't his nan tell him to 'crack on'? How the fuck could his nan tell him shit, she'd died falling down the stairs in 1970. He'd been eight and playing in the back garden when his dad sat him down to explain that Nan had passed. Why was he referencing his nan? "Crack on, crack on, lad, don't dither, c'mon, if you don't do something, you won't do anything now, will you?" She had a point, and cracking on seemed to be an option.

It was all a bit too much. He was a rag doll. He felt the hands again. His shirt was torn away, and he felt hands adding pressure to his chest, the stab of pain, and he drew a long sucking breath. The swimmy feeling from before was back, and he felt himself being turned on his side. At this point, he felt it appropriate to vomit four pints of Guinness, some Bruschetta, white wine and a Carbonara all over the firefighter holding the drip above his head.

"Fucking hell, mate," the Firebobby half choked. He was covered in vomit. "Fucking hell, mate," he poked the nurse who was holding the wad of bandage to the boy's chest. "Eh, he's puking his guts up, love, whatcha wanna do wiv dat?"

She looked round. "Nah, it's normal, he's in shock. Keep that line up; keep his airway clear; we need to get him out get him to the hospital."

His brain did a backflip, and he really wanted to laugh. The vision of Leslie Nielson and the scene from 'Airplane' rolled through his head.

"Hospital, what is it, doctor?"

"It's a large building with patients in it, but that's not important now."

He felt fuckin stupid. He was lying on the floor covered in his own blood, and now this. It wasn't how the night was supposed to end. But at least his left ear worked, and the vision was blurry but his left eye also seemed to have joined in and started working as well. As his nan had said, "Crack on."

She was conscious again; an oxygen mask attached to her face. She'd felt waves of nausea pouring over her, hot and cold. She was shaking, and the ambulance crew were fussing around. The ambulance swayed, and the belts holding her on the stretcher felt overly tight and uncomfortable. The lights, noise and movement were deeply unsettling. She was crying again, the tears rolled back into her hair. The crew had wiped the dust and blood from her face to assess her injuries. There was a needle in the back of her hand connected to a tube that ran up to a bottle of clear liquid; the bottle swayed as the ambulance rushed through the late evening traffic. Charring Cross Hospital was not so far, they'd be there in a few minutes.

Through the chaos inside the pub, the firefighters and ambulance crews and police assessed the living, the almost living, and the dead. Makeshift covers were placed over the faces of those intact enough to need them. They would count later that there were twenty-eight people killed in the initial blast, and four died later of their injuries. Forty-six people were now on their way to various A&E departments across West London. Some had just walked home…

He was on a stretcher. The off-duty nurse who'd attended him initially was by his side. They were on the pavement outside the pub waiting for the next available ambulance. Blue flashing lights gave everyone a sickly pallid glow, the light bouncing back and forth off the front of the buildings opposite.

"Alright, mate?" She asked.

No, he wasn't alright, and where was she?

"Who?" The nurse asked.

He muttered away, not really making much sense. The nurse leant in to hear, and as he spoke, small bubbles of blood formed on his lips. He could taste the blood and the vomit in his mouth. "The girl," he whispered.

The nurse looked back: "Not sure, mate, lots of girls, where was she?"

"Blond hair, blue eyes," he tried his best to remember her name but the cold wave travelling up his right arm had gained all his attention.

The doctor withdrew the needle, stepped back and nodded for the crew to load him onto the waiting ambulance. He did his best to remain in the world, but his consciousness was having a bit of a row with his abilities, and consciousness lost the battle. He bubbled a breath out.

They'd wheeled her into the A&E. Such as it was now, there was organised chaos. In only a few minutes, she was in a small side room. A doctor arrived to assess her and spoke briefly with the sister who was looking at the tag pinned to the front of her blouse.

The doctor needed to check for other injuries. A nurse bustled forward, all intent on getting things done in as short a time as possible. Taking scissors from the front of her uniform, she cut away the torn blouse, and neatly cutting the laces from her boots, she removed them. Next, she worked her way up the legs of her jeans, cutting all the way through the waistband on both sides of her pelvis. She then removed the remnants of clothing. The doctor checked her for signs of any obvious damage. He spoke briefly with the sister ordering more fluids and flashing a light in her eyes to check for the appropriate response.

'Bustly nurse' wiped more dust from her face. The doctor was busy feeling her stomach and around her ribs, her neck and checking her legs. Amazingly, other than the damage to her eardrum, concussion shock, small cuts and bruises, she was almost uninjured.

"What was her name?" He noted it down on a pad with an ever-growing list of names and addresses. Could she recall what happened at all? No, not as such. The noise and confusion, it was all too much to take in. The nurse finished wiping her face, arms, and hands. They got a paper gown and as they swapped the fluid over, they pulled the gown up her arms and attached the strings at the back. It reminded her of him helping her with her coat. Where was her coat?

"Where was he?" She asked.

The doctor looked puzzled. "Who?"

"He was right there," she mumbled a little, the doctor strained to hear.

The heat built in her face, and she felt the tears come again. They poured down her face, dripping onto the gown. Her nose was running, and she wiped it on the back of her hand.

'Bustly nurse' pulled some towelling from a roll on the wall and wiped away the tears and snot.

"Who was with you, Miss?" She asked. She felt the wave of emotion again, and she blew a perfect snot bubble as she tried to speak and cry at the same time. The doctor was filling a syringe with something; a small scratch on her upper arm, and a few seconds later, the world became warm and somewhat fuzzy.

"Where was he?" She asked again.

"He was holding my hand." She looked off into the distance as if he would be there somehow, waiting.

A police officer hovered by the door. She was pacing back and forth and occasionally glanced into the room to see if it was okay to speak with the girl. The doctor made a small shaking motion with his index finger and shook his head. "Not now, officer, sorry."

It was around two and a half miles from the pub to the hospital. It seemed Hannu Mikkola was driving the Ford Transit ambulance; they covered the distance and were outside the door to A&E in just over five minutes.

Porters and nurses were at the back of the ambulance. They bumped him down onto a trolley and the porter took charge to get the boy into the treatment area as quickly as possible. The floor of the booth looked like an abattoir: pools of blood, dressings and discarded equipment littered the area. A doctor pushed her way forward, looking at the wounds on the boy's side, and reading the blood-covered tag attached to the bandage. She understood right away the seriousness of his injuries. She asked if they had his blood type. Could they get that done and could she get the pulmonary surgeon as quickly as possible, please?

The boy's face was swollen on the right side, his eyelid closed, and the damage to that side of his face more extreme than the other. He'd taken the brunt of the force down the right side, at least three of his ribs were broken, and the lung had been punctured. His left arm had sustained a compound fracture to the Ulnea; they needed to get him properly stabilised before they could go any further. They'd used a portable defibrillator kit on him at the scene, and it was really only the sharpness of the off-duty nurse that saved his life.

Unconsciousness was losing the battle to remain in place. He opened his left eye and the doctor looked directly at him. The staff moved as if in harmony, and the boy could make out shadows and blurs of people.

He tried to speak again. "Where was she?" He asked.

The question felt really fucking repetitive at this point.

The doctor leant in. "Stay calm, try to stay calm."

A nurse wiped blood and vomit from the side of his mouth and the boy spoke again. "She was there, I saw her from the corner of the room." A single tear rolled back down into his hair.

The doctor had no idea where he'd been in relation to any of the architecture of the pub.

"Who are you looking for?" She asked. She made a motion with her hand and people froze, motionless as the boy bubbled out her name. He wasn't to know, but she was less than fifty feet away, being treated by one of the doctor's colleagues.

She was wheeled into a separate room, just to the side of the main ward, and close to the nurses' station. The waves of emotion had lapsed into a numb silence. The police officer had taken her name and address, and, as she lay there, they were trying to reach her parents. They wouldn't succeed. Her mother lived in the US now and her father was away in Switzerland on business; he wouldn't be back until the following Saturday. The house was dark, and though they rang the bell and banged on the door in only the way that the police 'can' bang on a door, it remained unanswered.

"Any other relations?" The sergeant asked.

"Not that we know of."

"Okay then, lad, onto the next."

They had 'deadograms' to deliver and the sergeant needed a strong brew with at least three sugars before he could face the next door knock.

The only people who knew where she had been were Rachel and the white t-shirt guy, whose real name was Daniel. Rachel was three parts of the way to waking up with a mind-bending hangover and wouldn't know of the evening's events until she turned on the radio in the morning. Daniel had heard the muffled bang, the sirens, the fire engines police cars and ambulances screaming down streets in the direction of the noise. He'd put two and two together, come up with five and rolled over into an alcohol-induced sleep. He'd wake up to the news that she was missing tomorrow, and he would realise that he'd missed the bomb by less than fifteen minutes.

The porter pushed the bed into the ICU. A ward had been converted for the seriously injured from the pub. If they grouped them all in one place, the staff could monitor events as they happened without needing to run to separate areas of the hospital.

The ICU nurse turned down the sound on the monitor, the rhythmic pulse crossed the screen, and he'd been noted as serious but stable. The operation of the damaged lung and the arm fracture had gone well. The ocular surgeon had removed a shard of glass from his right eye; by some chance, it had missed the nerves and had entered grazing the Sclera. He would probably not lose the sight in his eye, once the swelling had gone down, and when they could remove the stitches in his face, they'd no more. What they needed more than anything else was his name.

Chapter 6
Gathering

Her father had seen the news when he'd come in for breakfast at the Hotel in Bern. The Swiss TV channel showed black-and-white scenes of the chaos in London, the Swiss news reporter motioning towards the shattered pub front through the rain.

He'd had a father's sixth sense and had called the house from the hotel reception. There was no response, and for sure at this time on a Sunday morning, she should be home. He let the phone ring, the receptionist smiled at him briefly and went back to filing papers. Who could he call at this point? What was the name of that boy she was seeing? He couldn't recall. Didn't he come from the countryside somewhere? He wished he'd asked he didn't keep a note of all the voices that called her. She was very busy with the new show, and he'd been sure that the 'boy' would fade into obscurity once the show started and she was busy. It seems he wasn't right: hadn't they made a date? Who would know?

He flicked through his small pocket phone book, searching for the number of the production manager: if anyone knew, he would.

The phone barely rang the tired voice on the other end.

"Hello, Simon? Yes, this is Carl."

The voice on the other end of the phone seemed to snap to attention. "Ah, Carl, yes, how can I help?"

"Simon, you must have heard about the bombing last night, in town, and I can't reach her on the phone. Was she out with the other members of the cast?"

"Yes. They all had dinner and gone on to a club."

Was he sure? Bombing! Simon wasn't sure at all. They'd all seemed pretty certain that after dinner, they'd go onto the club in Chelsea. Could Carl call him back in fifteen minutes? He had to ring around a few of the crew and see if they had seen her.

The phone in Daniel's flat rang four or five times. He rolled over in bed, pulling the pillow over his head. He cried out, "Fuck, it's Sunday, please in god's name who was calling this time on a Sunday!"

He plucked the receiver from the cradle and pushed the phone under the pillow to his ear.

"Yes."

"Daniel? Simon."

"Yes, Simon, what the fuck?"

"Did you guys go to the club last night after the restaurant?"

"No, they went to a pub off the Brompton Road. Why, what's up?"

The breathing on the end of the phone had his attention. "Daniel, was she with you?"

Yes, he'd left with Rachel a bit before closing, and she'd stayed with the other lad who'd come to dinner that night. What was his name? Shit, he couldn't remember. Didn't he listen to Bowie and dress like an old-age pensioner?

Simon dropped the phone. Almost immediately it rang again. "Carl, she was in a pub on Brompton Road with some of the cast; they had left and she stayed with the boy she was with."

Simon reached across to flick on the TV and pushing through the channels, the news came up with images of the pub and the damage.

A grim-faced journalist stood in front of the building talking into a microphone. Simon had the sound down, but he understood.

"Carl, I'm sorry but Daniel tells me she was there."

The phone went silent. Carl asked the receptionist to make out his bill, and could they call a taxi please as soon as possible.

The receptionist picked up on the urgency in his voice. "Yes, sir, of course, where to?"

"Zurich airport."

She was on the phone to the taxi company, "Yes, as soon as possible, from the Hotel Schweizerhof. Yes, Zurich Airport, please as quickly as you can."

A bubbly red-haired nurse bumbled into her room, picked up the chart from the end of the bed, made a couple of notes and looked at the girl sleeping soundly in the bed. She'd been lucky. Some of the pub victims had died in the night, three, she recalled, and another one was hanging on.

The girl stirred. Her short blond hair made her features seem almost childlike, and the dark rings under her eyes had no real sense of belonging. She was far too beautiful to look so tired.

"How are you today, my dear?" Red Hair asked.

The girl wasn't sure. She had a small band using just a bass drum playing in her head, and she ached from every muscle and joint. Could she have another question, please?

Red smiled. "You're a lucky girl, you know?"

"Really?" She replied. Right now, she didn't feel so lucky.

"The doctor will be along shortly, dear," she trilled, "he's just making his rounds." Would she like a cup of tea? She wasn't at all sure, but the idea of a drink sounded good. Her mouth felt like something furry and smelly had slept in it. She nodded.

Red bobbled off to fetch the tea. She returned about five minutes later with the tea in a plastic cup. She had sachets of sugar, would she like some? She nodded a reply. Red ripped off the top, poured it in and stirred with a plastic spoon.

She hitched herself more upright, and the line in the back of her hand was deeply annoying: did it need to be there? Red nodded and fussed around to plump the pillows. The girl didn't know, but Red had seen her last year in 'The Sound of Music' and was a fan.

The doctor approached, and Red became a bit more self-conscious.

"Good morning, doctor."

"Good morning, nurse, and how is she?"

He looked from Red to the girl; she was propped up on the pillows sipping tea from a plastic cup.

He reached across to pull down the gown and place his stethoscope on her chest. His bedside manner sucked as it was really cold, and she felt herself wince.

"Sorry, my dear," the doctor checked his watch, "hmmm, I'm afraid you'll need to stay in for another couple of days. We'd like to keep an eye on you. It seems your eardrum is damaged, which of course will repair itself, but we want to keep an eye on you for the symptoms of shock. Do you understand?" She nodded.

Had the police been to talk to her yet? She shook her head. The effort to talk seemed to have left the room, and she didn't know where it had gone.

"Hmmm," the doctor muttered to himself. She was listening in mono and didn't catch what he said.

They had come to remove her drip. The needle had left a small hole and a bruise on the back of her hand, and Red had made sure to put on a sticking plaster. They bought some pills in small cardboard cups, and Red poured water into a glass so she could take them.

She felt awful. The world seemed to press from behind her eyes, and the numb dead feeling she had made her feel clammy and as if she needed a bath. Oh, a bath, that would be nice. She drifted away for a moment, but there was a scratching sound in the back of her head as if there was something important trying to get out. She didn't swear very often, but this seemed an appropriate time to start. "What the fuck do you want?" She asked. The scratch tore through the thin membrane of memory, and she snapped up in the bed.

The steady rhythmic thump seemed to come from inside his head. He tried to open his eyes but found that only the left responded, and it seemed to be full of gunk in the corner, and the eyelashes were stuck together. He attempted again. The gunk peeled apart and he looked up into the bright strip lights above his head. He wanted to move his arms, but one was bent at about ninety degrees and in a cast, attached to cords on a frame. There were pins sticking through the cast and it grabbed his attention. While that was taking his attention by the collar and dragging it that way, he'd lifted his right arm and the pain of doing so was like being punched by a train.

"Fuck me!" He'd moaned it out loud and the effort shot another '125 Special' across his ribcage. The voice was making some effort to grow. He'd try to relax and have another go. If only his voice would calm down and perhaps he could whisper.

"Hello, hello, sorry, but for fuck's sake…Hello," the 125 was back. It smashed its way down his cheek into his ribs and did a number on his right leg on the way past.

A face appeared above the bed. She had a light in her hand and was waving it in his eye. It did appear he only had one. He thought how lovely her skin was; she spoke with a Caribbean lilt to her voice; it was beautiful and soft. He tried to follow her movements, but any kind of effort had the 125 in full attendance. Her face swayed away, and he heard her speaking to another person in the room. The other face appeared. He tried with the softest hello; he didn't need another battering from the 125.

"Can you hear me?" He blinked, tried to nod, winced and the face went away.

"Can we increase his pain meds, please and make sure that he stays immobile? I'll make a note of the dose."

He felt like everything was filtered through cotton wool. The sounds and the numbness in his body. The ache in his head. It felt like he'd gone 15 rounds with Henry Cooper. Was he still around, Henry Cooper? He didn't know, but he was sure that he could still knock seven bells out of him, and had done so.

He was whispering her name, the sound barely audible, but Cammie, the ICU nurse heard the whisper, and she put her ear to his mouth. What was he saying? He was asking for the girl, the blonde girl. Had she seen her? Was she alive and where was she? Cammie looked down at him, a smile spread across her face and the beautiful skin glowed under the lights. She knew who he meant.

"She's here," she said, "I heard she was in the ward on the other level. She's okay."

She would go and find her, and yes, she would tell her he was alive. He tried to smile and say thanks and move his hand to reach hers all at the same time. The 125 did a double whammy pass, and the room did a neat rotational trick. He closed his one functioning eye, and as much as the pain would allow, he relaxed.

Carl was arguing with one of the staff from Swiss Air; couldn't they please put their correctness to one side, just for once, and understand his daughter had been caught up in the incident in London last night? The young man at the counter fussed through some notes. No, there was no room on the next flight; he'd double-check, but had he tried the British Airways desk?

Look, he'd sit in the jump seat, anything…he just had to get back to London. The young man picked up the phone; he switched from English to German then to French, back to German, and finally looked up at Carl, raising his eyebrows. He made a note on a piece of paper, he switched back to English; could Carl pay with a credit card? He could, he had a gold American Express card, and it really wasn't an issue. The young man nodded, speaking German back into the phone. He picked up another and spoke French to the person on the other end. He blinked, repeated the request in Italian and put down the phone. Could he have the card, please? He would take the payment, and Carl needed to hurry. They would remove the air bridge in 15 minutes. Yes. The gate number? Twelve. Carl picked up his case and hurried towards the customs and the gates. He had a jump seat; he'd have happily clung to the tail if it had gotten him home.

He hadn't been able to talk to anyone who knew anything in the police. He'd tried from the hotel, but nobody would answer his question. Could they not at least tell him the hospitals the victims had been taken to? "No, sorry, sir," all enquiries were through the officers handling the case. When could he speak to them? Not at the moment, they were at the scene. He hung up, his face flushed and his temper flailing around trying not to unleash itself.

She'd felt the flush of anxiety. Where was he? She'd no recollection of having seen him. Her memory was a scrambled mess of cartoon images, flicking, rushing scenes came and went, some in colour, others washed and in monochrome. The tears came; they felt hot and pointless, but they flowed anyway, and her nose joined the party to have a good run. She was looking for a handkerchief or some tissue, or toilet paper, anything to wipe away the mess she was making on her face.

A face was at the doorway; it was Cammie, the ICU nurse. "Can I help?" She proffered a hanky, and the girl wiped away the tears and the seemingly incessant flow of snot.

Cammie was smiling. The girl looked into her eyes: Cammie had the most honest open face and she was smiling. The smile was one of relief, and she rushed the words out: she'd seen him, yes, he was alive, and he was in ICU on the other floor. Yes, he regained consciousness this morning. Yes, he was serious but stable, in a lot of pain; he'd lost a great deal of blood. No, he couldn't move as such: he had broken ribs, punctured a lung, and damage to his face and his right eye. She wanted to see him. The thought of seeing him washed whatever pain away she felt; she was consumed with a sense of need. Would Cammie help?

It was against regulations. Cammie had doubts, but the girl was sure. If Cammie would just walk her part of the way…No, she couldn't do that. She pleaded. Cammie caught the moment, it hung briefly in the air, and she decided that it needed to be taken down and used for a good purpose.

She wanted to swing her legs over the edge of the bed. She was incredibly sore, and the effort involved took more out of her than she could imagine. Cammie lifted her feet and helped her to swing around in the bed. Here, the biggest issue so far raised its head; beneath the backless robe, she was naked. She'd not really noticed and had no recollection of having removed her clothes. She couldn't go wandering through a hospital showing her bottom. She tugged at the gown. Cammie caught the concern and removed the cardigan she was wearing over her uniform. She was a bit taller than the girl, the cardigan fitted like a dressing gown. Who'd know?

She had no shoes. The cold floor wasn't a concern. She'd spent enough time barefoot on stages and if she could just get to see him, it would be worth the effort. Cammie had her elbow. She was chatting away, talking about the events of the night, how she'd been on duty since two am and she didn't remember eating. Had the girl eaten anything at all? No, she'd had some awful tea that smelled like a plastic cup and some drugs that made her feel giddy. Other medical staff buzzed up and down the corridors, all consumed by the need to be elsewhere. The lift arrived and Cammie pushed the button for the appropriate floor.

Her nerves were doing small somersaults in her tummy, butterflies arrived, did some loops and left, leaving her feeling washed and tired. The lift pinged to let them know they'd arrived. Cammie took her arm again, guiding her gently along the corridor. She swung open the door to the ward. The girls' senses were assaulted by the number of people, the machines going 'beep', and bottles hooked up to the motionless bodies. She took a short breath in; she wanted to cry again. She wasn't such an emotional person, why could she not keep her emotions in check? Cammie walked her to the bed.

He lay motionless. His left arm was held up by a cord to the frame above the bed, and the cast was from his elbow down to his wrist, small metal pins stuck through the cast at different points. He had a bandage around his head and a gauze covered the right side of his face, the cheek swollen and yellow. The tears came and paid another visit. She sobbed, gripped his fingers in her hand and squeezed. Cammie had seen some emotional shit in her time as a nurse, but this was a milestone, and she cracked: she put her arms around the girl's shoulders, and felt the power of the sobs as her shoulders rose and fell.

He sensed motion, sensed the pressure on his fingers. His left eye did its level best to open. He had fuzzy vision, and he blinked two or three times to clear the gunk attached to his lashes. The pressure increased, he felt drops falling on his face and for all the world he couldn't understand. The vision did another loop and cleared. The blue eyes bored into his eye, channelled their way through the clouds and mess, reached deep into his being and plucked him back into the world.

She kissed him, as gently as a butterfly landing. The tears fell into his eyes, their salty content making him blink. She sobbed again, kissed him as lightly as she could and whispered his name. He joined the crying party, the tears flowed back down to the pillow, running past his ear and soaking the bedding behind him.

"Please," he begged, "please don't make me blow my fucking nose!"

Her eyes seemed to collapse in on themselves, and she laughed. She bent forward again and planted another kiss on his lips. She made a slow breathing exercise as if she was about to sing, no sound came, just utter earth-shattering relief.

Finally, they had his name. She'd filled them in on his identity, and the sister called the police officer waiting in the hospital canteen to come up. He'd taken the information, and once the wheels were in motion, the Met called the Bedfordshire mob, and a car was despatched to Spring Lane, number 67, wasn't it? The young PC in the passenger seat nodded, and the dog van accelerated through the town, out onto the main road that led to the village. As they approached the river bridge, the driver made a note of a fertiliser bag hanging from a tree just next to the bridge. He'd passed it a couple of times and thought it could be a distraction. "I must pull that bugger down," he thought.

The boy's dad had listened to the news on the radio. Wasn't the boy in London yesterday? The lad's mum looked, took another sip of the instant coffee and nodded. Ah, but he was seeing that girl, no? Sometimes he went away for weekends, and they didn't hear a thing. Sometimes he went away for weeks, and they never heard from him. His dad had a growing sense of unease, a twitch had developed in his eye, and he wasn't at all comfortable with it.

The dog van pulled up outside 67, a blue Saab 99 stood in the driveway. 'Dog Van' knew the car, he'd seen it around and being a nosy bastard he made a check. It belonged to that noisy little shit's dad, the lad with the Yellow Yamaha. Now it belonged to the dad of a little shit who'd almost been killed in a pub bombing in London. Funny old game, ain't it?

He eased his bulk out of the van. His colleagues were always mystified about how he ever caught anyone. They reckoned he starved the dog, and it would hunt down anyone with the command 'sandwich'.

Walking past the Saab, he approached the house, front or back…decisions, decisions. He really was a bit of a useless wanker, everybody thought so.

The boy's dad had seen the van pull up. He'd seen the blue light on the roof above the hedge row from the window. The twitch in his eye gave another flutter; he was ex-military and emotions were not in the order of ever being shown, but his face flushed a little. His mum looked up, "What is it?"

"It's the old Bill," his dad motioned towards the window. His mum's heart took a jump, and she spilt coffee on the tablecloth. The fucking 'magpies' never bought good news now, did they?

'Dog Van' banged on the door. He knew the boy's dad had seen him heading for the front, but enjoyed the knock anyway, always makes 'em jumpy, see.

Harry opened the door. "What is it, mate?"

'Dog Van' looked up. He hated being called 'mate', but anyway, he'd enjoy the next thirty seconds or so as he spooled out the bad news and watched as Harry paled and gripped the door handle. "Look, here's a number you're supposed to call, they have all the relevant information."

No, he didn't know where he was. He did, actually, but being a nasty fucker he thought he'd make 'em suffer a bit. Fucking council house pikeys.

Harry thanked him for letting them know. He wasn't sure why nobody had just called them once they found out, but 'Dog Van' had enjoyed the game. He glanced at the windscreen of the Saab, "Tax is due on that in a couple of weeks," he said.

"I'll make a note." Harry felt his face redden, the words boiling in his chest, but the boy's mum was there, shaking. She'd heard 'Dog Van' dish out the news. "Where was this number?" Harry passed it across. She was fumbling to find the key for the lock for the rotary dial on the phone. "For god's sake, Harry, what have I done with it?"

Harry was trying to get the key in the ignition between the seats. He unlocked the Saab from reverse, as the boy's mum got in. "He's in ward ten, Charing Cross Hospital." Harry knew the way already, much of London was imprinted on his brain. His right foot trembled as he pushed the accelerator peddle down. The Saab nosed out of the drive; Harry shot off down the lane, hooked left at the bottom and headed for the M1. If he kept his foot in, he reckoned they could be there in an hour and a half. "Fuck me," he thought, he'd kill birds with farkin stones today and get to see Nick an' all.

Chapter 7
Hello, Daddy

The Boing 737 had turned on finals for Heathrow. Carl sat in the rather uncomfortable pull-down seat at the back of the cockpit. The captain flying was on the left side, and he was chatting away to air traffic as the co-pilot turned dials and switches, and tidied up the cockpit for the landing.

Carl was anxious to get on the ground. Obviously, his daughter had no way to contact him. He very rarely left forwarding numbers for her. She'd grown up independent and her mother had left some years before to live in New York with her girlfriend. He never got passed using that term: it grated somehow. Perhaps he was just getting old. He had to contact her when he landed, six hours difference, she should be awake by now.

But where was his daughter? He'd call the number again when he landed; surely someone must be able to tell him by now.

The PC had taken the details for the boy, and at the same time, he'd passed her details to the duty officer. Even though her name and address had been noted the night before and a car despatched, she'd somehow fallen through the cracks in the ensuing chaos, and her details misplaced. Someone was due to get their balls in a mangle for that, he was pretty certain. He took another sip of the vending machine hot chocolate, secure in the knowledge it wasn't him.

Carl approached the customs official holding his passport out, ready for inspection. He'd spent what seemed like an eternity waiting for his luggage. A police officer armed with what looked like a machine gun stood near the desk. The customs guy looked at him blankly. "Anything to declare?" Carl shook his head. The customs guy glanced from Carl to the document, back to Carl, closed the passport and handed it back, twitching his head in the direction of the exit. Carl was itching to go, but it crossed his mind to ask the officer with the gun if he knew who he should contact for information regarding the victims of last night's bomb.

The 'Bobby' had the weapon in a sling around his neck, and his right hand rested on the pistol grip. His forefinger pointed to the side of the trigger guard, his other hand lightly gripped the forestock, his eyes motioning back and forth as people made their way through the customs point and out into the airport. Carl approached, and the 'Bobby' waited for the usual pointless 'is that loaded' question, but this guy was sweating and looked pale and a little panicked. The 'Bobby' was an old hand; he'd seen that look before.

"Excuse me, sorry, but I need to ask for information: I believe my daughter was in that pub last night, the one on Brompton Road."

Carl had Bobby's attention at this point. He pulled a walkie-talkie out of his jacket, spoke into it briefly, and looked back at Carl; could he have his name? "Yes, of course, Nyman, Carl Nyman." And his daughter's name? "Sofia, the same surname."

Carl fidgeted. He wasn't a nervous man, very matter of fact, and he kept his emotions in check at all times, but his emotions were making a bid for freedom and he wasn't sure he'd built a tall enough fence.

"Sofia, did you say, sir?" The 'Bobby' looked at him, his finger poised near the transmit button on the radio.

"Yes, Sofia Nyman."

The Bobby confirmed with the voice on the other end of the radio; the tinny voice crackled through, and the Bobby strained to hear. "Yes, sir, he's here sir, yes, I can walk him out now."

"Would you come this way, Mr Nyman, please?" The officer took his arm and started to guide him towards the exit.

"I do have news, sir, your daughter was taken to Charing Cross Hospital last night; she spoke with an officer this morning. Yes, sir, all things considered, she's very well, I believe."

Carl let out a breath; he did his best to check the wayward emotions, he'd knocked them back off the fence and he'd resumed his normal composure.

The 'Bobby' motioned him towards a waiting Rover SD1 police car; the two officers inside looked back as he placed his case on the back seat. The 'Bobby' leant forward and passed the information to the two officers in the front. The driver had the engine up and running, and the Rover peeled away from the spot with the tyres doing their best to keep a grip on the road.

"Blues and twos, I reckon Dave, don't you?" Passenger 'Bobby' nodded, flicked a couple of switches and the familiar 'neeeh naaaaaah' sound of a police car wailed out into the London sky. He reckoned it was about twelve miles to the hospital. Punching the Rover past the Sunday traffic, he reckoned on doing it in less than twenty minutes. Nineteen minutes and thirty seconds later, he screeched to a halt at the hospital entrance, the big Rover ticked and pinged as he switched off the engine. "My colleagues are waiting for you inside, Mr Nyman; I do hope your daughter is okay." Carl looked back at the driver. He'd done his best to keep what remained of his breakfast in place on the journey.

"Thanks," he muttered and exited the car. The clutter of people outside surprised him; cameras pointed his way, flash bulbs, and the milling press folks looked to see if he was anyone important, they could grab a scoop.

The Met had set up a reception point for people enquiring about family and friends who may have been involved in the pub bomb. They definitely wanted to call it a bomb at this point, although there hadn't been the usual coded message from any of the known terrorist organisations to say they had planted it.

Carl approached and a young police officer looked up; could she help? Carl explained he was looking for his daughter Sofia. The young woman looked down to check a list. "Miss Nyman is on the fourth-floor ward six, sir, I'll ask my colleague to take you up." An officer stepped forward. "This way, sir, you can leave your case with the officers here." Carl's emotions were back at the fence; they'd bought wire cutters and meant business. He felt sick again and his left knee had developed an unhealthy wobble; he took a bat to the emotions, but they were wearing helmets, and the blows just glanced off.

The Saab joined at J14 of the M1. Harry pressed hard on the accelerator, and the chunk of Swedish engineering punched hard down the slip road. He was doing over 110mph by the time they got into the third lane. Harry was gently leaning backwards and forwards in the seat, willing the car on. The boy's mum, Chrissy, sat motionless in the passenger seat, her mind was spinning loops. "Why?" was a word that kept popping up; she batted it away, but it was insistent, and like a game of 'whack a mole' she hit it back, but there it was again and again. "First Nick, and now this, but why?"

They were at the bottom of the M1 in forty-five minutes. Harry swung onto the North Circular. In his head, he was visualising the turns to take, he'd go in via Park Royal, then Ravenscourt Park; if he ducked right just before the Great West Rd, he could miss a bit of traffic and it would take him to the road outside the front entrance. Chrissy had gone silent at this point: she'd lost the game of 'whack a mole', and 'why' pinged up and down for the next thirty minutes. Harry pulled into the front of the hospital: there were police cars everywhere, TV crews with cameras pointing pointlessly at the building. An officer put out the flat of his hand to stop the blue Saab. "You can't park there, sir."

Harry had a hand out of the window: "Mate, my boy, last night, the pub," the words were spat, staccato. Harry had poured out a ton of adrenaline on the drive, and it was washing around in his system, and having a lot of fun. Harry not so much so.

The officer wanted his name: Harry Brennan. The officer consulted a clipboard. "Ah, Mr Brennan, can you park there," he pointed at an impossible gap between a Mini and a Ford Escort police car. Harry tutted, his eyes briefly rolling up. "Out you get, Chrissy, I'll get it wedged in." Chrissy was out. She had a handbag in the crook of her elbow, and she was really in need of the toilet: the mug of coffee wanted out, she'd have to hang on. Harry nudged the Saab into the space, lifted the lever on the gear shift and locked it in reverse. The officer was waiting. "This way, sir."

Carl wanted to run up the stairs, but the officer had the lift door held open, and once inside he pushed the button for the fourth floor. The lift made its customary 'ping' as they arrived. Carl was by this point attacking his emotions with a chainsaw, but they refused to die. The officer was a little unsure which way her room was and stopped a red-haired nurse who was humming her way along the corridor. "Miss Nyman's room please, they said ward six?" Red bubbled with self-importance. "Oh, Sofia, she's this way." Could she ask who they were? Carl cracked; no she bloody well couldn't, just take him to his daughter!

Sofia was back in bed. After her excursion to see the boy this morning, she was incredibly tired, she'd slept, but it had been fitful. She had flashes of memory that startled her awake: she could smell burnt hair, and visualise the look on the man's face who'd fallen on her. He looked incredibly surprised, but then he had a piece of door frame sticking out the back of his head, so surprise would have been high on the list of looks to carry off.

Red had been in to check on her a number of times. She kept looking at her and her bubbly smile and demeanour were now coming across as annoying. Sofia had realised she probably knew who she was, and for all the world, at this point, she wanted to remain unknown.

Harry was at the desk, spilling out the boy's name and details. The officer looked and checked on the list. "Yes, he's on the fifth floor, ward ten, in the ICU I'm afraid. Let me call the duty sister." She picked up the phone, but Harry was already on his way to the lift, Chrissy trailing along behind.

"Harry, Harry, slow down, Harry."

He didn't wait to be shown the way; he waved the officer away impatiently. "Please, my boy," he muttered.

They reached the fifth floor, and Chrissy stepped out of the lift, scanning for the door to the ward. A piece of A4 paper was sellotaped to a door, and in black marker, it was written 'Ward 10 Temp ICU'.

Harry wanted to barge right in, but Chrissy checked his stride. "Hang on, love; I think we need to knock." Tapping lightly on the door, Chrissy stepped back to wait. Harry had, by this point, lost control of the twitch and looked for all the world like he was having a fit of some kind, which probably wasn't so far from the truth.

The door opened and an incredibly tired-looking black girl asked if she could help.

"We're looking for Rone?"

"Rone?" Cammie asked.

"Brennan, Ronan Brennan," Harry said. "We're his mum and dad."

Cammie did her electric smile face, and the tiredness seemed to take a step back into the shadows for a moment.

"Of course, he's sleeping at the moment, but if you want to come across, I can give you a few minutes. He's heavily sedated for the pain though, so please understand if he can't say much." Chrissy was thanking her, gripping Cammie's arm as she led the way. And there he was; the arm in the cast, bandage around his head and the gauze over his right eye.

Chrissy thought he seemed so incredibly small and was surrounded by monitors, and had wires and tubes connected to him. Harry felt his knees bend a little. He'd caught service at the end of the Korean War and had seen a lot of broken people, but this was his boy. Cammie left them. She'd see if she could find the doctor in charge of Rone.

Sofia was aware of two figures at the door: one looked incredibly familiar. "Daddy," she muttered. "Daddy?" Carl stepped into the room. The emotions were through the fence and attacking hard. He had tears on his cheeks, and he came towards the bed, bent forward and kissed her face, his hands reaching around the back of her head to clasp her into the crook of his neck. He kissed the top of her head countless times. Took a machine gun to the emotions and leant back.

"Darling girl, what have they done to your hair?"

"Looks terrible," she laughed. She was covered in small abrasions, bruises and was wearing a borrowed cardigan, but her dad had spotted the hair.

He scanned the room. "Oh, dear, this is quite terrible. I must call cousin Paul and have you removed to his clinic."

She shook her head. "No, Daddy, they should let me out tomorrow, I don't want to move, and *he's* here."

"Who?" Carl asked. "The boy?" Had she been with him? What had happened? The questions started to pour out and became a flood, then the Victoria Falls. She couldn't cope, the tear factory sounded the buzzer for overtime, and her emotions lost their own battle to stop a rampage.

In his head, Rone was peeling through the bends into the village, the left footrest of the bike scrapping along the tarmac as he cranked the Yamaha into the corner. The left, flick right, downshift, the left again and rolled the throttle as he was in the village. He was sure he could hear the crackle of the exhaust pipes, and he blipped the throttle to downshift and roll into the pub car park.

Why was his mum there? She was talking a lot, her voice had a slight midlands twang to it, and she'd occasionally make the word bus sound like buzz.

But no, he was sure he could hear her. His senses opened a door and checked if it was safe outside; it seemed to be okay, so they stepped out. He felt his consciousness returning, it was swimming very slowly from the deep end of the pool; it would get there in a moment.

"Rone. Rone, love, it's Mum." She took the index finger of his right hand in hers and gave a little squeeze. "Rone, love, it's Mum and Dad, we're here."

"Rone, boy." Dad's voice cut through the last few feet of the deep end and he opened his eye.

His dad took a moment to check his voice. He didn't want to crack any kind of blubbing nonsense, the Yanks did all that.

"What's happening, lad?" He tried to sound casual as if Rone had been to the shops and forgotten milk.

"Dad, Mum," he tried a weak smile.

The mix of whatever drugs they had him on, had him a little 'trippy' and he wasn't 100% sure they were real. He'd been on his bike five minutes ago.

"Alright son." His dad got as emotional as he was ever going to get and made to tussle his hair. He was a bit rough, and Rone took a beat and waited for any trains to show up. "Sorry, boy."

Chrissy had sat down. She just continued to stare at the lad in the bed. His brother Nick looked in poor shape, but this…'whack a mole' briefly returned, she dismissed it with a wave of her hand as the doctor arrived.

"Mr and Mrs Brennan?" She didn't want to speak in front of the boy, but Harry was impatient to hear the news, good or bad. Rone was a scrapper; he'd be fine. The doctor listed his injuries: the punctured lung, the broken arm, ribs, the piece of glass that had been removed from his eye, and the fact he lost so much blood. He had a rare blood type, AB negative, and they'd been delayed getting transfusions into him.

"How much blood?" Chrissy asked.

He'd lost about 20% and had gone into hypovolaemic shock. His heart had stopped at the scene, and his life had been saved by a very courageous off-duty nurse, who, though injured herself, had taken charge of the scene, and taken a defibrillator from an ambulance and used it to save Rone's life. They did expect to move him from the ICU in the next few days. The police were keen to speak with survivors, but the doctor had ordered them to stay away. Had Mum and Dad spoken with them at all?

Carl sat on the edge of the bed. He'd sent away the officer who had asked if his DI could come and speak to Miss Nyman. Carl had looked at her. She seemed very tired, but the DI was very keen if he could just have a moment. Sofia nodded: "It's okay, Daddy, they've been trying since this morning."

Ten minutes later, Detective Inspector Jacks was making himself as comfortable as possible in the plastic chair next to her bed. Detective Constable Parkinson hovered at the end of the bed. Jacks found him a bit annoying and sent him off to bring tea and did they have any biscuits? He'd not had tea for at least thirty minutes, and tea was far too wet without something to dip in it. Parkinson wasn't sure. Jacks gave a disproving look and asked him if he was indeed a detective. He was. "Then go and detect some tea and bloody biscuits, son."

Jacks took out a black notebook and needlessly licked the end of a pencil.

"Sorry, Miss Nyman, I don't want to trouble you for too long, and thank you for taking the time to see us." He noticed her father hovering in the corner of the room. He was pacing steps and appeared to be counting the linoleum floor tiles, and not stepping on the joints.

"Do you think you can remember where you were in relation to the explosion? We are trying to piece together the location of people at the time the incident happened." Who was she with? Sofia took a moment, calmed herself, and as if taking her place in a scene from a play, she stepped into the role of a witness.

Yes, she was with her friends. They had left and her 'date'…she stumbled briefly…No, 'boyfriend' had gone to the bar to get more drinks. Could she remember what they were drinking? Was it important?

"No, not very, just curious."

"Gin and tonic and Guinness. Rone…"

"Rone?" He asked.

Yes, she knew him as Rone, although his real name was Ronan. Yes, Ronan Brennan. He had paid, returned, sat down, they chatted, and they…no…*she* decided it was time to leave. Where were they going at this point? She hesitated. Her father looked across, an eyebrow raised.

"Home," she replied, they were going back to her home. Carl's eyebrows came back from orbit and he gave her something of a 'look'.

DI Jacks was making notes. His brain clicked, ticking away, something had kicked it in the shins, a distant memory, but it wasn't sure why it had been kicked at all. Why did they decide to leave at that point? Had they finished their drinks? She was unsure, but Rone had. She remembered standing; he helped her on with her coat. But in relation to the blast, they were heading for the door, almost there. Carl stopped mid-step and looked, and an eyebrow was looking for the end of the runway again.

"Okay, Miss Nyman, one last thing. It's not important, I don't think, but we found your bag and the remains of your coat. Do you remember taking your coat off again?" No, she had her coat on. He, Rone, had helped her on with it.

Jacks made a note again. "Okay, Miss."

"Please, call me Sofia," she said. "Miss makes me sound like my Aunt Caroline."

Jacks almost cracked a smile. In the meantime, Parkinson arrived with tea, a packet of Jaffa cakes and some sachets of sugar. Jacks looked at him with a look only a long-served copper could use. "Biscuits, I said. Those are cakes, and it clearly says, 'Jaffa cakes,' not 'Jaffa biscuits' on the packet." These young coppers. The service is going to the dogs.

Chapter 8
Well, I Never

Red had been stung by the harshness of Sofia's father. She was muttering to herself as she headed back to the dispensary to collect the various medicines for the patients in ward six.

She was only trying to be kind, and she'd made a point to take extra care of Sofia Nyman; who did she think she was, anyway? She'd only been in a couple of musicals, she had no right to be that pretty and that talented, and her father had been so rude. Red's brain was spinning into 'I'll make you pay' mode, and as she stomped her way along the corridor, she noticed a skinny guy wearing a blue anorak hanging around outside the locked door to the wards. He motioned with a nod of his head, he smiled and waved. His skinny face had far too many teeth in it to be healthy, and the round glasses propped on the end of his nose gave him an almost comedic look, but he was far from funny, and his intentions even less amusing.

Carl had left; he was heading home to collect things for Sofia. She desperately needed something to wear: the backless gown was beginning to fall apart, and poor Cammie had left her cardigan and had been too busy to collect it.

She had been quite specific: the underwear, the socks, which sweater, and could he bring her toothbrush? Oh, soap, and yes, the white training shoes, and the sweat pants; yes, the third drawdown in the dresser.

Carl had spoken to her mother: she seemed less than concerned and had been her usual 'colder than cold' self. No, she wouldn't come. Yes, she appreciated their daughter had been blown up in a bombing, but she was, according to Carl, 'okay'. She would be in London later in the month, she'd see her then. She hung up, Carl was left doing 'goldfish impressions' into the mouthpiece.

Sofia had slept again. The day was drawing to a close, and as the light faded, she felt drained and tired. She had tried to get up to see Rone again, but Cammie had finally been able to go off shift, and she didn't know if she could sneak back into the ICU without her.

What was it about Rone, why him? From the first time she'd seen him in the pub sitting with his friend, and how he'd brushed off the reaction of the crowd in the pub that night, she'd been somehow drawn to him. He had the kindest face, and his big brown eyes with their almost feminine long eyelashes. She could get lost in those eyes; she loved looking deep into them. She wasn't aware of the effect of her looking so deeply had on him!

He wasn't really her type; did she have a type? She had dated lots of theatre types on her way through drama school, nothing serious, but she was drawn to Rone: his quirky dress sense, he made her laugh, he had no idea who she was, and his reaction when he'd seen her at the rehearsal…All went a long way to add to the attraction. But he'd been gentle and kind; no desperate uncomfortable moments of fumbling: it added to his aura of 'being cool'. Sleep called at that point: it had made a point of being quite forceful, and she slipped into the hands of Morpheus with no resistance at all.

The events in the outside world followed the path that normally happens after such events. The 'red top' papers had shouty headlines about the IRA, with banner headlines proclaiming them as cowards and murderers. The TV news had various reporters and experts talking about the terror threat; the number of dead had risen to thirty-two, three victims had died in the night, and another had succumbed to his injuries this morning. People should be vigilant, and report any packages or bags left in public spaces; the security forces were on high alert, and a number of soldiers had been posted around potential targets.

Mrs Thatcher had made a statement condemning the bombing; she would not negotiate with any terror organisations, and any group resorting to planting bombs in public places to harm civilians was cowardly in the extreme. She would have those responsible hunted down and brought to justice. The Home Secretary had called a meeting with the head of the Metropolitan police, the chief of staff for the armed forces and the head of British Intelligence. They must understand that incidents like this would not be tolerated while he was Home Secretary. Did they understand? The commissioner of the Met, David Mc Nee had set up a task force, and Mr Whitelaw must understand that these things take time.

"Nonsense," Whitelaw had retorted. He'd had enough terror on the streets of London with the Iranian embassy siege. He wanted the full weight of the law brought down on the heads of those responsible. Mc Nee pointed out at this point that they actually didn't know who was responsible: doors had been knocked in, 'contacts' in the various terror organisations had been contacted, and those who would normally have shouted responsibility for such an act had remained silent. They were, for all intents and purposes, flying blind.

Red was due to end her shift, and she was heading to the staff room to collect her things and head home. It had been a long day and the number of patients had doubled as a result of the bombing. That, along with the normal intake of the sick and injured, had left her feeling footsore and tired. But in her mind, the incident with Carl Nyman was chewing away at her; it had decided that it needed to bite through any kind of reason and have a good chew on a bit of revenge.

She grabbed her bag and coat from the locker and changed out of her black shoes into a pair of comfortable trainers; she signed herself out and headed for the door.

The blue anorak guy was still hanging around; as she pushed the button to release the door he stepped forward. Could he just have a word? If she just had a moment…She stood in the door: it hadn't swung shut yet; the electronic lock was not activated.

Who was he and what did he want? "My name is Colin Wood," he was with the *Sun* newspaper.

She tutted. "Not interested." But if he could just get a short statement… "Anyone of interest inside?"

Red's mind stopped chewing for a moment, took in the question and decided another good bight might just be enough.

"Interest?" She asked.

"Well, yeah, you know…" He left the question swinging from a loose nail, hoping it would fall and knock Red into answering.

"Sofia Nyman is inside." Colin's internal Rolodex did a quick rotation through the names of interest at that time.

"The actress?" He asked.

"Yes," Red nodded.

"Is she bad?" Colin did a little Skippy step as he asked; part of him hoped she was, it would be a good copy, and it would have his name on it.

"Not so bad," answered Red, "concussion, cuts and bruises. She'll be fine; they should send her home tomorrow."

Colin salivated; his overly full mouth couldn't cope with the amount of saliva he was producing and he made an odd sucking sound as he breathed in.

"Can I see her?" He asked.

"No, she's sleeping, none of the patients can be disturbed," and she'd be sacked if they found out.

"I can make it worth your while." Colin made a little gesture with his thumb and forefinger. Any sense of what was the correct thing to do at this point had been chewed away, revenge was sitting back with a full belly, waiting for cigars and a possible brandy.

Red glanced back. The corridor was empty, the night shift was not out on the ward yet and handovers were being done by sisters in charge, junior doctors and the night shift nursing staff.

"Come with me."

She stepped aside and Colin shuffled through, he produced a camera from a satchel that was hanging from his shoulder.

Red looked. "No photos, I'll get sacked!"

Colin made the odd sucking noise again. "Ah, just a quick snap."

The door to Sofia's room was open. Colin was looking back at Red to see if she was paying attention. Red had him padlocked into her gaze. Colin could see the girl in the bed, her head turned towards the door. He could see her face, her hair was very short; he wanted to ask if they had cut it due to any kind of injury, but instead, he lifted the camera and hit the button. The shutter fired probably ten times: he had his shot.

Red pulled him back from the door. "Stop it! I told you no!"

Colin went all sucky teeth again and was heading for the exit. Tomorrow's headline splashing across the inside of his mind: *West End starlet maimed* or *West End star critical.* It didn't matter really: either way, he'd got his scoop. And Red was just dumb enough to believe him.

Harry and Chrissy had spent some moments with Rone. He'd drifted in and out. Chrissy wanted to give him a hug and tell him it would all be okay. Harry sat motionless; his mind spinning cartwheels. The one side of his mind was calm and plotting any kind of revenge it could, the other part of his mind was having a good deep think about what Rone had been doing that evening...And who was this girl he'd become so involved with?

Chrissy asked the same question. "Did he tell you about her?"

Harry shook his head. "Nah, love, don't know anything. Didn't she live in Lambeth or Chelsea?" Rone never spoke much about girls he dated, and Chrissy had started to just say, "Yes, dear, I'll tell him you called." There had been a few this year, but this girl had phoned more than others, and Rone would always climb as far up the stairs out of earshot to speak with her. Chrissy didn't know whether she liked that or not.

"We should go, love, see if we can see Nick and let him know what's happening." Harry stood up, stroked the side of Rone's face, and ran his fingers into the hair sticking out the top of the bandage.

"Alright, son," he whispered. "You fight on, boy." Chrissy kissed him lightly on the cheek, and they turned to go.

DI Jacks was in the lobby talking to the officer at the reception desk. They were sure they had almost everyone accounted for, and he was thumbing through the names on the list. A name stood out: Brennan. Where did he know that name from? Brennan. The 'shin-kicking' started again. His brain was rolling back through a shit load of names, faces, events. Was he a wrong'un? It span on. Brennan. No, hang on…spin back a bit…Brennan, Lance Corporal Brennan. Wasn't he on Gloucester Hill in Korea? Nah, his brain refused the information, had another good shuffle around and rotated back to a time when he was a sprog trooper with the Royal Fusiliers. Hadn't Harry Brennan been in charge of the section that held off the Chinese with a Bren gun and a handful of blokes? What was that operation called? His brain span out a series of names. Pimlico, that was it. Operation Pimlico.

At that point, the lift had arrived and the ping had DI Jacks turning to take a look; and there, stepping out of the lift, was a face he hadn't seen for the best part of twenty-eight years. Still lean, still fit. It couldn't be, could it?

He stepped forward. His brain was taking a break from shuffling events, and it was now very nosey and looking forward to seeing what happened next. It looked up: here we go.

"As I live and breathe," he reached out his hand, "Harry Brennan?"

Harry took a moment and looked from Chrissy to the slightly chubby bloke in the bad suit who was offering his hand.

It took a moment for him to put the face back nearly thirty-odd years. It hadn't been chubby and wearing a terrible suit. It had been shit scared in a trench, being told to pass another fucking clip for the Bren gun.

Harry did that thing that old soldiers did; his back went straight, and his thumb found the seam on the outside of his trousers.

"Jacks, private Jacks. Well, whatever are you doing here?" He took the offered hand and shook it. Jacks looked into the face of his old section corporal, and the years rolled back.

Jacks had seen Rone's name on the list. He offered Harry and Chrissy a seat. The part of his brain where he'd been in a trench with this man sat back, leant against the back of the trench and listened.

"So, Harry, your boy, how is he? They tell me he took a fair knock."

Harry was still coming to terms with seeing Jacks again. "Sorry, what?"

"Your boy," Jacks offered again.

"Ah yeah, he's knocked about a bit." Jacks actually knew the extent of his injuries but didn't want to add a comment.

"So he was seeing that actress, Sofia Nyman?"

Harry looked blank. "Who?"

"Sofia Nyman. She's a bit of a star in the West End apparently."

"Really?" Chrissy asked. "He never tells us anything…actress, star…Last time I saw him, he'd knicked his grandad's hat and was heading out the door to the station."

"Actress!" She exclaimed again.

Chapter 9
Time

Inspector Jacks had finished sifting through the wreckage at the pub. The forensics team, the counter-terrorist forensics and the army bomb disposal teams, along with various 'experts' had examined the site. They'd pinned down the location of the device itself. It had been left on a stool at the bar, probably in a sports bag. They'd found the remnants of a black Adidas bag. Parts of the detonator had been recovered, parts of a six-volt battery, and some wiring. They were struggling to pin down the make of the explosive, but one theory offered by one of the Army team reckoned it was a form of RDX, which was a military explosive, commonly used in large bombs during WWII.

Jacks stood next to the remains of the bar. His thought process was to understand the direction of the blast, which didn't seem as obvious as it should be.

Parkinson was at his elbow. "Guv?" Jacks remained silent. His thoughts were replaying the carnage he'd witnessed the morning after the explosion, and his thoughts were not keen to have Parkinson's intrude. He held up a single finger, it waved in a back-and-forth motion, and Parkinson knew to shut up before he got told to shut the fuck up. He was shuffling the images back and forth. He could see where Rone had lain, and where Sofia had landed and the two other victims had landed on top of her. The general consensus was that they had soaked up the main blast, acting literally as 'human shields'. The one victim had been in the region of sixteen stone, and he had stopped the real blast force from reaching her; a large part of the door frame from the bar had embedded itself in the back of his head. The other victim who shielded her was another larger gentleman; he was also killed by a piece of what turned out to be a chair that had hit him in the back of the neck, killing him almost instantly.

Rone was a bit more of a mystery. He'd been between two other victims, and apparently, he'd turned back to look for Sofia when the device detonated. If Jacks could recall his notes, he'd looked back over his left shoulder. The blast had separated the two people who were there, and Rone had taken some of the blast down his right side. A lot of glass fragments were found in his side; a piece of a beer tap had pierced his side and broken his ribs on the way through to his lung. The bar top had been lifted and had broken in two parts, the one part killing three people on its way back down, and breaking Rone's arm and trapping him on the floor.

There were of course other victims than Sofia and Rone, but their circumstances of survival were a little particular. They had, in all senses of the word, been fucking lucky. He'd spoken at length with the officer who'd found Sofia, but he had no recollection of removing her coat. Had it been blown off in the blast? The mystery of this was nagging at the back of his mind, and it kept pecking like a woodpecker…just wouldn't give up. The explosives blokes reckoned that, given the blast, and the fact a lot of the victims were found naked and in just their shoes, it was probably the blast. But something in his mind wasn't having it. Peck, peck, peck.

Sofia had been released from the hospital a couple of days after the incident. Her father had collected her and they'd caught a cab home. The journey from the hospital had not been without its drama.

She was restless to get back and see Rone, and Carl worried at the level of apparent infatuation she was showing. Sofia had no such worry; she was worried for Rone. She'd managed to get back up to see him, and in the days after he'd been more lucid and the bruising on his face had reached the yellow, purple stage. She'd wanted to kiss him a lot. He'd asked for something to drink and she'd found Kia-Ora in a vending machine, stuck the straw in the little box and held it while he drank. Her thoughts bounced around in her head. She couldn't settle and the slightest noise made her jump. She had not been able to go back to rehearsals; she'd broken down on the stage, and Daniel had helped her home.

Her father had called cousin Paul. She'd been to Harley Street to his clinic, and cousin Paul had his psychiatrist book her some sessions. Her brain kept sending unwanted waves of emotions her way and she'd had enough of them, but like junk mail in the post, she could do nothing about her brain ordering another pair of furry winter wellingtons.

Rone had become her reference. It was now a month after the incident, and he was in a normal ward, bouncing off his internal walls to get out. He was convinced he could go home. She wanted him to go nowhere, she wanted him right there, with her.

Carl had to go away again on business. No, it couldn't be put off. He'd arranged with Paul to have his assistant call by every evening to make sure she took her 'quiet time' pills. Carl needed to go back to Switzerland to finish up the remains of the deal he'd been making.

He thought she looked more frail than normal. He hated to leave; the doctors had told him she needed peace and quiet. She should stay in and rest. She'd actually had enough of 'resting' but understood.

She'd seen Rone every day. "No, Daddy," she needed to see Rone every day.

Carl had finally met 'the boy', as he called him. He looked dreadful and Carl couldn't see why she wanted to be with such an ordinary boy. She'd lost patience with her father, and in the last weeks, she'd had moments of hysterical loss of control around him. In his mind's eye, he should have liked to stay but the deal in Bern was the biggest thing he'd pulled together in some time. He'd had to leave the last time he was there due to the bomb, and the clients were less than pleased: they were the sort of people he needed to keep happy. All this added up to something big, bigger, in fact, than his daughter's mental state.

Rone saw her coming. It was cold out and she had on a big coat, and a woolly hat pulled over her ears. She pulled off the hat and coat as she walked towards him. The hair had remained short, almost cropped. He loved the cute elfin look, but she looked pale and incredibly frail. He knew she wasn't eating properly, and he felt the need to wrap her up and put her somewhere warm.

His arm was still in the cast. They removed the pins, added another cast and it itched like mad. His ribs and the wound to his side had healed pretty much, and they did think to send him home in the next few days. Cammie had visited him almost every day she'd been on shift, and they'd become firm friends. She'd taken to calling on Sofia and taking her mum's home-cooked food; she often sat with her to make sure she ate. Cammie had mentioned to Rone how withdrawn Sofia had become; she was worried about her. Rone too: in his head, the battle raged to ask her what was happening, and what he could do. 'Happening' was losing to 'can do' by some distance; he felt a bit helpless. Here she was: she bent to kiss him and produced a Mars bar from behind her back. He grinned back. "You're hungry, aren't you?" He nodded. It had been at least forty-five minutes since he'd eaten: the 'rat' was in full attendance.

"What will you do when they send you home?" She asked.

"Dunno. Mum and Dad are asking the same. If I go home, I'm too far from you, and I don't want to leave you here alone." His internal dialogue had gone so much better and he was sure Robert De Niro played him well.

"Look, Daddy is away. Why don't you come home with me and we can see what happens? I don't want to perform at the moment and I'd like to take care of you."

His internal dialogue was adding in lines from Alec Guinness at this point, something about Jedi knights and princesses!

The following day, the doctor had called down to see him: she felt he was well enough to leave. The doctor who'd spent the most time treating him was called Sarah. They'd gotten on 'first name terms'. His eye had healed and the swelling was long gone, the small stitches they'd put in had been removed. No lasting damage; the ribs were still sore and the damage to his lung had him breathing like his granddad who smoked at least fifty fags a day. But she was sure he could go. Harry had popped in every couple of days. He was often in London with the lorry, and could always find a place to leave the trailer and come see him. When was he coming home?

His mum missed him and they wanted him back home. The trouble was: he didn't want to go home. He wanted time with Sofia. He was asking questions to himself about staying in London with her. Both sides of his brain were trading blows, and every now and then his mum would pop up and try and separate them. He was coming home. End of!

So that was settled; he could leave tomorrow. He'd shuffled his way to the phone in the hall to call her. Could he stay with her? Could she come? "Of course, 10 am?"

Okay, she'd arrange a cab and pick him up.

The second call was a bit more fraught, and Chrissy was really upset with him. "Look, love, you need to be here, we need you home. Your granddad is asking after you, and Nick is home now and could do with the company."

He could hear Nick in the background making lewd comments about him shacking up with Sofia. Rone cracked a smile; his brother was such a dick, but it was good to hear him feeling well enough to take the piss.

"Mum, no. Look, no, Mum." His brain did a handbrake turn, slid into a parking spot and shut off the engine. He let his mum go on for another few minutes. Beep, beep, beep. The phone conveniently asked for more change. "Sorry, Mum, gotta go." Click and she was gone.

In the past month, Sofia had suffered at the hands of the press. The day after Red had let Colin Wood onto the ward, the paper had printed the front page with a picture of her sleeping in the hospital bed. The headline had screamed: *Teen actress torn apart by terror bombing*, and when Carl had arrived to pick her up, he was mobbed by reporters and photographers eager for their shot. "Mr Nyman, this way, sir, Mr Nyman!"

They had tried to find a way out of the hospital without leaving by the main entrance, but the press had ambushed them coming from the entry to A&E. They were chased in the taxi by paparazzi on scooters, eager for a shot of her. Once home, the attention had become relentless: they banged the door, posted notes through the letter box and besieged the house for at least five days. But the interest soon petered out. Some 'nutter' up north had killed some girls with a hammer, and the 'red tops' decamped up the M1.

Cousin Paul had arrived with 'pills' and had calmed her down, but the chemical effect was merely just glossing over the damage inside. Paul knew she needed real help: he'd called a psychiatrist, Gretchen Neil, and she'd been to see her for several consultations. But Gretchen wasn't helping: she couldn't break through the wall that Sofia had built inside.

She tried to return to rehearsal, but instead of being a healing point, it added more stress. Sofia was losing the internal battle to remain herself; in her head, the battle raged to fight back to normality, but abnormal was winning by a 'knock out' and a 'standing count'.

It had not been hard to find the source of the original photograph. Colin Wood had thrown Red under the proverbial bus to save his own ass, and Red had been fired. DI Jacks had wanted to find some obscure law to charge her with, but he ran out of options. She'd suffer at the hands of her own vanity and her career in nursing in the UK was over. She'd crossed a line of trust, and had nobody else to blame, except Sofia Nyman: the blame lay squarely at her feet, fucking bitch.

She arrived with the cab, and Rone was waiting with some carrier bags of belongings: his pyjama bottoms (the top was too much, mum), his wash stuff and a few other clothes that Chrissy had brought down for him. Sarah was there, and Cammie. He was more than just a patient for Sarah; he'd become something important, she'd pushed hard for different procedures for him and kept him on the ward when probably he should have gone home a couple of weeks before. This skinny kid with the smile and brown eyes, and the attitude to life that seemed to be full of bouncing back from so many different setbacks had found a place in her soul. She shouldn't get attached: remember the rules. Fuck the rules; they were there to be broken.

The cabbie looked back. "Where to, Miss?"

"Portland Place, please." The cabbie nodded and looked twice in the internal mirror. Didn't he recognise the couple in the back? The lad looked much skinnier than before, and the girl looked tired and pale. Surely it couldn't be the same couple as a few weeks back.

"You okay, Miss?" He asked. Sofia eyed him with some suspicion. Of course, why shouldn't she be? "Nah, 'nuffin', Miss. I just remember you and the lad from some weeks back. His 'barnet' was a bit shorter, but, you two looked appy, and that's rare in this day and age."

She picked up that the cabbie meant no harm, 'fine thank you' she smiled back and relaxed in the seat. Rone was oblivious; it was his first time out of the hospital in just over a month and he was soaking up the change of scene.

27 Portland Place came up on the left side and the cabbie pulled up to the kerb. She passed across the note and advised

to keep the change. The cabbie had seen the lad moving slowly and obviously in pain.

"Good luck to you, Miss," he offered.

Sofia glanced back; the blue eyes flashed back to their normal ability to bring daylight to a dark London day, and the cab rattled away from the kerb.

"Up you come," she said, guiding him slowly up to the front door. Rone hadn't known what to expect: the place, the location. But he was back to not really knowing what to expect; his nerves were back, and the self-confidence had slipped a little, grabbed a convenient handrail and was hanging on. The hospital had become his refuge away from normal life. Cammie and Sarah had become props to lean against when the hardest of times arrived.

Now he was with Sofia, on the threshold of her home. A few weeks ago, he was supposed to be here under different circumstances and he'd be happy to swap a bomb blast with the battle that raged inside his head right now.

Sofia slipped the key in the door, and helped Rone inside: "Tea?" She asked.

"Oh, mate!" He double-checked himself. "Sorry…Sofia. Cammie called everyone mate!" Sofia smiled in the most honest way he'd seen in some time.

"Yeah, a brew would be great." She hummed as she filled the kettle and dropped a 'builder's' tea bag in the cup.

"Toast?"

"Oh, you're ticking all the boxes. If you have Marmite, I'll marry you tomorrow!"

"Would you?" She asked; her face almost without an expression.

Rone looked back. His senses told him an important moment had arrived; he'd better not fuck it up. His senses were right, co's no matter what happened next in their young lives, Sofia had fallen head over heels in love with Rone, and nothing else mattered right now except him.

DI Jacks was at his desk, such as it was: a mess of note books, papers and general chaos, but his chaos. He'd called an old Sapper mate; he'd spent time as a bomb disposal guy during the war, did a tour or two in Northern Ireland hooking bombs out of lamp posts.

Jacks pushed a cup of NATO across the desk (coffee, milk lots of sugar), and passed him the report. He spent a bit of time digesting the contents.

"Nah, mate, don't add up."

"What do you mean?" Jacks asked.

"Well, lad, if she was shielded, and she was, by the fat blokes, then her jacket would have stayed on. Plus, the 'Bobby' who got to her reckons she didn't have it on, so how did it get in the corner of the bar?" He took a sip, recoiled slightly at how bad it was; took another sip, readjusted the taste parameters and carried on. "Look, no matter and I mean, no matter how you look at it, the jacket was taken off after the event. Talk to the 'Bobby' again, and the nurse. But you know something? There's something not right about the bomb, mate."

"How so?" Jacks asked.

"Well, mate, normally when you plant a bomb in a building to cause casualties, you pack it with shit, old nails, bolts, bits of metal to cause maximum damage to the humans inside. Looking at this report, there's none of that. It almost looks like a shaped charge, but pointing the wrong way."

This piece of information wasn't lost on Jacks. He filed it away in his ever-growing list of shit he'd have to look at later. Shaped charge. But right now the filing system had churned out something else Sapper Bob had said.

"Fuck me," Jacks thought, "who would be farkin cold enough to rob dead people?"

He looked at his watch, motioned to Parkinson that tea was urgently needed, picked up the phone and dialled the number for Harry Brennan. "Harry, remember that time we got blowed up by that mortar?"

"Not something you forget, fella. What's on your mind?"

"They came in the trench, didn't they?"

Harry muttered something about little fuckers. "Yeah, mate, they did. We played farkin dead, and they went through our stuff, robbed shit, like, and bayoneted a few lads with wounds."

Jacks nodded. The tea arrived; he took a sip and waved vaguely at the chair for Parkinson to sit. "Harry, I checked the notes for Rone. We went through his things; he said his watch was missing. The explosives guys reckon it wouldn't have been blown off. Was it the one the yank pilot gave to you when we fished his arse out of trouble on the hill?"

Harry was rolling back the veils of time. "Yeah, fuck me. He always wears it. Hamilton, square face. He fucking loves that watch."

"Is it worth much, Harry?"

"Dunno, Jacks, but it went through a lot. Who'd knick a watch off a dying kid?"

"Yeah, exactly," Jacks thought. "Who the fuck would do that?"

He picked up a red Moleskin note book and chased a number. "Ah alright, Harry, I'll keep ya posted. Keep yer elbows in."

Harry hung up; the revenge section of his brain changed up a gear and pressed the accelerator to the floor.

Sofia had made the tea and toast. Rone devoured it almost without breathing out. Amazing! Did he want another slice? No, what he wanted was a bath, without anyone coming to see if he had drowned!

She laughed. "Seriously, you're here with me, in an empty house and you want a bath?"

Self-doubt and a lack of the right answer knocked with some fury on his door.

"Well, babe…sorry," Cammie again; she called everyone babe. "I didn't say I wanted a bath on my own, just a bath without anyone barging in to see if I was okay."

She smiled. The blue eyes did that trick that they hadn't done for a while and deep-dived into his soul. He felt they'd crossed a bridge and that they somehow belonged together. No matter what happened next, the time with Sofia was the most precious he'd ever have.

The lights from the street shone through the bedroom window and Rone shifted position. Sofia was asleep with her head on his chest, and his left arm really hurt. But he didn't want to wake her. She was sleeping so soundly and looked incredibly fragile. Her skin was opalescent in the light, and she was breathing with a slow steady rhythm. He was sure it was the most soundly she'd slept in some time, and he wasn't wrong. His mind drifted back to the pub on the Downs, how he'd seen her, the eyes and the smile. It felt like a million lifetimes ago and he struggled to hold back the emotions. Laying here with her now, he felt the enormity of the moment again, and the release of weeks of pain and suffering rolled out of his eyes as salty tears.

"I love you," he whispered.

"I love you too," she whispered back.

She opened her eyes, did a deep dive, read the writing that was backwards on the mirror, smiled and kissed him.

"I know," she said, "I know all your secrets, Rone Brennan. Everything you've written on that mirror is mine to keep."

She kissed him again and fell asleep. It was the first time she'd slept without the drugs. The only drug she needed, apparently, was right here, living and breathing next to her.

Chapter 10
Moments

"Breakfast?" She was standing in the doorway with a tray, with toast, a pot of coffee and marmalade. He blinked his eyes open.

"Hello you," he smiled. She was wearing his 'Clash' t-shirt, a pair of woolly socks and a really big smile; he really thought that she had more colour than the day before. The eyes sparkled, and her face had an almost familiar glow. He hitched himself up in the bed, and she slid in, balancing the tray as she did so.

He had no top on, and she looked at the long scars on his side; there was still a purple tinge to the wounds, and she could see the marks from the stitches.

"Are you still very sore?" She asked.

"Not so much." He didn't want things to be about him, and he made a note to be as positive as possible around her.

"What did you want to do today?"

"Well, other than polishing off this toast and seeing how you look without that t-shirt, not so much!"

At that point, as they so often do, the phone rang. They let it; it stopped and started all over again. "Persistent, aren't they?" It could only be someone she knew, as the number was ex-directory, and had been changed a couple of times after the intrusion by the media.

She picked up. "Hello?"

"Ah, good morning, Miss, er, Sofia, it's DI Jacks."

"Oh hello, how can I help?"

"Well, I have some new lines of enquiry and I was hoping you may be able to help. Have you seen Rone Brennan at all? I tried the hospital, but he's been discharged."

He actually knew exactly where Rone was; he'd spoken to Cammie, and she'd enthusiastically blabbed the whole story.

"Ummm, Rone? Well, yes, he's here with me at home."

Would they mind coming to the station? He'd like them both to look at some evidence. He'd send a car. Rone was listening in, nodded and shrugged his shoulders.

"No problem," she replied.

"Okay, car there in about forty-five minutes."

"That's fine," she replied.

"Okay, see you then Miss." Damn, he just couldn't help himself!

She removed the tray and placed it on the floor. He was looking at her, and she was absolutely beautiful. His self-confidence was barging around knocking self-doubt around with a cricket bat; self-doubt was on the floor feeling sorry for itself. She slipped out of the bed, and walked slowly across the room, peeling off the shirt as she went. She giggled, dropped it on the floor, and ran for the bathroom.

The investigation was not going well. The combined forces from different departments could find no answer to who had planned and planted the device.

Normal lines of enquiry had run into dead ends, and one of the 'spooks' from MI5 had sources inside some of the more obvious terror organisations. At least one of them flatly denied they'd been involved, and doubted the others would be so brazen to attack a quite pointless pub in London; after all, Chelsea barracks wasn't so far away. They could have targeted a 'squadie' pub and killed something legitimate.

Jacks had put Sapper Bob in touch with two of the counter-terrorist bomb squad guys. Could he go through the evidence with them again? Something he'd said about a shaped charge, and the explosive being military grade RDX had bells ringing in their heads, and Sapper Bob had been around a few tricks and nasty things that went bang. He'd outlived most of his old team. A good reason for that: he knew when to run like fuck, and when to stay and defeat the threat.

A metallic dog-shit brown coloured Ford Cortina pulled up outside the house in Portland Place. Rone and Sofia were putting on coats and getting ready to go. Rone had no jacket and Sofia had dug through her dad's wardrobe to find something he could wear. She delicately slipped his left arm through the sleeve of the Macintosh, and he struggled his right arm into the rest of the coat.

"Fuck me," he laughed, "I look like Inspector Clouseau."

It went well with the jeans and his new Vans.

Jacks was in the lobby to greet them. He was startled by how much Rone looked just like his dad had during the Korean War, took him a moment to process that. He nearly called him Corporal; his brain did a little shake and corrected itself.

"This way please, how are you both? Rone, you look well all things considered."

Sofia was on his right side, holding his hand. They threaded their way through the labyrinth of the police station and down into the evidence room.

Jacks had some boxes open on a table, and he took a moment to stop them both.

"Look, I'm about to ask you to look at the remains of your clothing and possessions from the night of the incident." He didn't want to use the words 'bomb' or 'bombing'. 'Incident' made it sound softer somehow, or so he'd been told.

"Miss Sofia," for god's sake…now he was mixing 'Miss' and 'Sofia'. He'd get a grip in a moment. "Can we go through this box first?" There was a white plastic sheet on the table next to the boxes; he put on latex evidence gloves and started to lay out the items from the box. The first thing out was her grey coat; then, the remains of her white blouse and jeans which had been cut off when she was in the emergency room, her boots, the laces still neatly cut through but in the eyelets, her socks, and, lastly and very carefully, her bra and pants. Next, her bag. He reached in and brought out the contents: lipstick, some tissues, her purse, loose change and a small pocketbook with names and addresses.

"Sofia, if I may ask, are all the items here yours?"

She looked. The clothing was scorched in places and blood spattered; the room went a bit swoopy and Rone felt her sway a little. "Hang on, mate; can we get her a chair?"

Jacks got her a chair and he placed a hand on her shoulder.

"Sorry, Sofia. I understand this is not easy, but we need to verify these things are indeed yours, and that everything is here."

The room seemed to jump. She smelt the burning, felt the weight and the struggle to breathe, images flashed past in a hurry; they weren't stopping for tea and a chat, they needed to be elsewhere.

She sat up. "Okay, it's okay. Now, everything seems to be there."

Could she check the bag? He passed evidence gloves and she slipped them on. Inside the bag was a small pocket. Normally, it would have held her house keys on a little gold Snoopy key ring, but it wasn't there. She rattled her brain and tried to think back to the moments before the blast. Rone was finishing his drink, his head tilted back, draining the last of his pint; she'd kissed him moments before, and they were about to leave. She'd reached into her bag, taken the key and put it in her coat pocket, she wasn't sure why. She took the coat from the table and checked the pockets, but the key was not there. Her brain did a spool back and forth; she played out the moments again. No, she'd put her key in the pocket. Did it get lost in the blast? "My keys," she said, "my keys are missing."

"Are you sure, Sofia?" He asked. She rummaged again.

"Yes, a gold Snoopy key ring and the keys to the house."

They were not there. Jacks made a note; he picked up a phone on the wall and called Parkinson. Can we check all the listed items found at the scene of the bombing? He was looking for a gold Snoopy key ring with a set of house keys. Yes, he knew it would take a while, but again, "You're a detective, go detect some help and get them involved."

"Okay, Sofia, thanks." He mentally scrambled the information into the allotted space. "And that's all that's missing?"

Rone spoke up. "No, no mate, your necklace, sorry." Sofia looked at him.

"Your gold necklace, 'Star of David', you had it on all night. I noticed it 'cause it wasn't so big, and I just wondered if you were Jewish." She'd forgotten all about it; a detail mashed into the blur of the evening events. It was a gift from a friend. No, she wasn't Jewish; it was a symbol of their friendship, the dark-haired girl in the pub that night on the Downs, Anne Marie.

Jacks was back on the phone. "Yes, also look for a gold 'Star of David' necklace. No, not big, fine chain; the symbol about the size of a five-pence piece."

"Rone, let's take a look, shall we?" Sofia gripped his hand.

"Okay, crack on, mate, let's have a look."

Jacks lifted out the Herringbone 'granddad' coat; it was bloody and torn, a large piece was missing from the side and the left arm missing, the bloody remains of his red check shirt, an almost unrecognisable piece of a white t-shirt, blood-soaked suede boots with no laces, the vintage jeans cut off in a similar way to Sofia's. His granddad's flat cap, socks, and a pair of pants with Scooby Doo motif. Sofia laughed, Rone visibly shrank. Her eyes flashed out a 'how were you going to sneak those past me', and she laughed again.

Jacks caught the moment and chuckled away. "Nice pants, son."

Rone shrank and then shrank some more.

"Now, Rone, anything missing? We didn't find a wallet, no ID."

He reached into the box and found a small bag containing some change and fifty quid in cash; the notes blood-stained and discoloured.

Rone looked at the pile of rags. He did a little shrug, a little jolt of pain went up his side, and inside his head he felt doors being opened and banged shut; behind each one a different image, bang, slam, bang, slam. Hang on, his watch. He'd asked Jacks before if they found his watch.

"No, son, wasn't there and they didn't find it in the pub." This was all that he arrived at the hospital with. "I know it's not a great thing to ask, but any recollection at all?"

Rone was trying to get the picture back on a grainy black-and-white TV in his head. "I reached up, just after I was blown over. I felt myself reaching up."

"Are you sure?" Jacks asked.

"My right arm was up in the air, I felt it. I had some odd sensations after that; my nan, Sofia, sticky, wetness…Nah, after that, I was pretty fucked and it's all bits and pieces of images."

"You're right-handed son, yes?"

"Yeah."

"But you wear your watch on your right side?"

"Yes, I do. I'm a bit cack-handed. I use a knife and fork the wrong way round as well."

Jacks noted it down. It went in an allotted space amongst the chaos.

It all went a long way to confirm what Jacks first suspected. Someone had robbed dying people, but why the house keys and not the address book and handbag? Just the keys, and really bits and bobs, the necklace, the watch. They had to go through the survivor's list again, bring the poor buggers in, and make them go through the same process these two bloody kids had been through. Fuck. Gonna be some long hard days in that.

He'd called a few 'toerags' the other day after speaking with Harry, just to put the word out on the street he was looking for the boy's watch. Now he was looking for the necklace as well. It took Parkinson and the 'volunteers' he'd detected three days to go through all the lists of items found: no keys, no necklace, no watch. They interviewed the survivors; oddly, none of them had things missing as such. Some things were destroyed, but no watches taken, no necklaces, just Sofia's and Rone's. Why was that? The woodpecker was back, tapping away; it was a relentless bastard, and he could do without it.

Jacks had been to see Doctor Sarah. She'd been one of the first to treat the boy, and he wanted to know if it was possible he'd been able to lift up his arm, given the extent of his injuries. She wasn't sure. The woodpecker arrived, drilled away for a few minutes. Rone had deep lacerations to his side, the ribs were broken, and a piece of the bar tap was sticking out of him. "I mean, anything is possible. The body will do incredibly complex things, even when we're dying." She couldn't say for sure, but if she had to make an educated guess, she'd say no;: the trauma and the shock, the fact Rone was just a few minutes from being dead at that point. Peck, peck, peck.

Parkinson had a lead on the watch. He'd had a snitch looking around the pawn shops. The watch wasn't an everyday thing and there was something that made it unique: engraved on the back was the pilot's name, 'Lieutenant Paul Forsyth.'

"Guv, we have something; there's a pawn shop up near the Elephant and Castle, run by a sharp little fucker called Albert Singer. He's a dodgy fucker so we'll have to watch our step. We need to go mob-handed co's he's a bit of an handful and maybe tooled up."

Jacks was reaching for the phone. Ten minutes later, they had backup in the form of some lads from the firearms squad, and were on their way. The pawn shop was set back off the street. Singer had arranged mirrors so he could see anyone coming from any direction; he'd had cameras, but they kept getting knicked. The fucking irony wasn't lost.

They'd do a 'hard knock', no fucking about. This bloke was a bit of an animal; he'd done time for armed robbery and GBH. They'd gone with an unmarked Ford Transit and the dog-shit brown Cortina. The lads in the van were pretending to make a delivery. They were going to park by the street entrance and fuck about with boxes, just to keep him distracted. The other lads were with Jacks and Parky. Jacks branched off, the others should go through the door, he was going round the back. As with all plans, it went well until it was executed.

Singer had got the windup and got suspicious about the van; the next thing, all hell broke loose as they tried to beat his door in with a sledgehammer. He was out the back and over the wall in a well-practised escape route, running down the alley to his Jaguar which was sat at the end of the road, keys in hand. He'd just fuck off for a bit, lay low, fucking old Bill. He made it as far as the end of the alley, and as he burst into the road, a fist slammed into his face. Jacks had gotten in the way. He was shaking his hand. "Fuck me, mate, I reckon you bruised a knuckle or two."

Singer was blathering on the floor, the blood from his broken nose running into his mouth. "You cunt, you fucking piece of shit cunt!"

Jacks had heard it all before. "Alright, son, calm down. Let's go and have a little nosey round the shop, shall we?"

Parky appeared. "The Guv still had the fucking balls when it mattered, eh? Fuck me," he thought. "He's gone up a step in my book. I thought he was just a grumpy twat, now he's a grumpy twat with a right hook."

One of the boys got Singer in cuffs, and they marched him around to the now-destroyed door. Usual pawn shop inside: lots of knock-off shit and dodgy-looking knives, cameras knicked off tourists and lots and lots of gold tat.

"Now then, son," Jacks had little patience, his hand hurt and he had no time for scrotes like Singer. "I'm looking for a very particular watch, and I hear you have it."

Singer spat blood on Jacks' shoes. "Fuck off!"

Parky and the boys looked the other way as Jacks reached across, took Singer's nose between his thumb and forefinger and twisted; the already broken septum cracked some more.

"Fuck me, son, that don't sound good, eh."

Singer cried out, "Fuck, fuck fuck off!"

Jacks added a bit more pressure. "Nah then, son, we can do this all night, but I've promised the boys a curry and they are fucking hungry."

"Fuck!" Singer was breathing hard. "Top draw, cabinet behind the counter."

Jacks nodded and Parky opened it up. "Square face Hamilton Emerson boss, gold back, reads Lieutenant Paul Forsyth."

"Very good, lad. Now, I need a gold chain with a gold Star of David, about this big," he made the shape of a five-pence coin.

Singer was living up to his name by now. "Glass cabinet, on your left," he spat again.

Parky had the necklace in his hands.

"Right," Jacks said. "Arrest this fucker for receiving, and then what we want is the fucker who brought it in here."

Singer visibly snapped. "No way, mate, I ain't no grass. I ain't grassing on that fucker. I'm as good as fucking dead now, fuck off."

Sofia and Rone were eating Chinese takeaway sitting on the mat in front of the fire. She'd put on an album by Aretha Franklin and opened a bottle of red wine taken from her dad's wine rack: Valpolicella. Rone was getting into this wine thing. He quite liked it, made him feel mellow, and a little bit pissed. He hadn't had a drink for over a month, and this had a direct line to the slightly tipsy side of his brain. The fire, the music and Sofia; it was all a bit dreamlike, was it real? He'd wake up in a while and find out he was actually dead and she was part of some trick, but the 'trick' poured him more wine and kissed him on the head.

"You really need to sort out your barnet." She laughed so hard. "Hahaha, I'm talking just like your dad!"

"Talking of dads, when is yours back exactly? I don't really want him to come home and find me in bed with his daughter!"

She wasn't sure, and he shouldn't worry. She'd had boys stay over before; Daddy didn't mind as long as she was somewhere safe. Rone felt a twinge of jealousy; he wasn't that way inclined but…shit! "Sofia?"

She smiled at him: "You mustn't worry. I can see in your eyes the questions. You can ask what you like, Rone, and I'll ask back. There have been girls before me, I'm sure there will be girls after me, but I'm with you now, and you're all that matters. This small space in time we have represents a moment of passing; I'd like to come out the other side of this with you intact and by my side. I'm 18 years old, but I can't help feeling that something in our souls brought us together. We should just celebrate the now; we've already lived our nine lives in one night."

Aretha rolled into 'Ever changing times' and Rone reached up, put his hand on the side of her face and kissed her, softly and with as much genuine love as he could.

"What have you done?" He asked.

The blue eyes took an everlasting dive, and they entwined on the floor in front of the fire.

Chapter 11
Message

Sapper Bob had spent some time with the counter-terrorist lads. They'd been through as much of the evidence as they could, and Bob had all the photos of the scene laid out on the floor of their office. They had tried to lay them out as a collage, to piece together the scene of the floor of the pub. The photos of the walls and interior of the pub they had pinned to a large board on the wall, and it brought the scene together as a whole picture, rather than just individual pictures. Bob was looking intently at the wall. One of the counter-terrorist lads, Chris, was at his side.

"What's up, mate?"

"Hmmm," Bob nodded, hmmm'd again and looked from the floor scene and back to the wall.

"Nah, mate, the more I look at this, the more it isn't a device for blowing up people."

Chris looked back at him. "How would you come to that conclusion, Bob?"

"Well, son, you pop the kettle on, get a brew going and I'm gonna explain."

Terry and Chris had some years of explosives knowledge obviously, but Sapper Bob was a bit of a legend in their world;

so once the brews were made, they got around the table with Bob.

"Okay, lads, look, do you see the way the ceiling is punched up? And if we look at the way the bar top went vertical, not sideways at first, but vertical; the secondary part of the 'bang' pushed the shock wave in a vertical motion, before it became a shock wave that spread out. The wave that killed people came in a sideways, downward motion, bouncing back off the ceiling. Nah, this pub was rebuilt in the 50s and they used concrete lintels, not wood. So when the wave hit that, it didn't deform, it pushed it back down. See what I'm getting at?"

If Chris had nodded any harder his head would have fallen off.

"Nah then, boys, we're looking at a farkin 'shaped charge' for blowin' a hole in something, not a bomb for killin' people."

Terry was looking hard at the pictures. "Bob, what's that?" He pointed at a round bowl-shaped piece of metal about a foot in diameter, that was driven into the floor. Bob had on two pairs of glasses at this point.

Terry piped up. "Mate, we thought it was a bowl for a plant."

Bob sat back and took a sip of NATO. "My boy, I reckon that is a directional shape charge bowl. It's farkin crude, but you boys is switched on, and that fucker right there would create 'the Munroe effect'. Like I say, farkin crude, but whoever built this, knows what they are doing. Nah then, where the fuck is it?"

Rone was due to have his cast removed. He'd travelled to Charing Cross with Sofia, and they were waiting at the outpatient department. Rone had called Sarah and asked if she had time for a coffee. She did, possibly. She'd see, and she'd come down to see him. They'd arranged to meet Cammie after for a bit of lunch. Rone did lunch now, not dinner.

He was called through, and the nurse was waiting with a large pair of cutters to chop away the plaster. Rone had his arm up on the table and she chomped her way through, peeled it off and took a massive helping of his arm-hair with it! He went a bit red and blushed.

"Sorry," she said. "That's always a tricky bit."

Rone was looking at his very thin, white pasty arm: there was a large scar that ran from his elbow almost to his wrist. She wiped away the plaster residue and cleaned around the scar.

"Okay Mr Brennan, I think we're done."

"Mr Brennan is my dad," he grinned and she caught the drift, smiled, and pulled back the curtain. She was a busy lady and had no time to chat.

Sarah met them in the waiting room; she was pretty busy but wanted to say hi to them both. Rone was showing off his 'chicken wing' arm, making Cammie and Sofia laugh. Did she have time for a quick coffee? She glanced at her watch. Yeah, go on, she'd make time.

"How were they both?" She thought Sofia looked 100% better than she had. And, "Rone, I do believe you've put on some weight." She had a cool smile and was using it to full effect. Rone grinned back; all the takeaway food they'd been eating. Cammie sat back and watched the dynamic; she knew how much Sarah cared about not only Rone but Sofia as well. Made a change, doctors were normally so far up themselves.

Sarah turned to Sofia, was she still seeing Gretchen? No, she didn't see the point. Rone was with her, and Gretchen kept asking the same questions, it wasn't helping.

"And how are you sleeping?"

Sofia looked her in the eyes and glanced at Rone. "Together!" she replied.

Sarah got the point. She couldn't council these two; they were flying it together, and for sure it seemed to be working.

Sapper Bob had called Jacks. "Mate, we need a chat, co's I reckon you're off in the wrong direction with the terror thing."

"Really?" Jacks spun it up in his head. "How so, Bob?"

"Well, I don't reckon the bomb was meant for the pub. We discovered a shape cone, to direct a blast; it's pretty crude but effective."

Plus, they'd nailed the explosive down to RDX, which was normally used in munitions. It can be made to go bang in the right way, obviously, but takes knowledge. Terrorists normally go for plastic C4, or Semtex; the RDX thing had him a bit baffled, either it was what was available, or they couldn't get C4.

"Isn't a shaped charge normally for tanks and armour, mate?" Jacks asked.

"Well, yeah and no. You can point a charge in any direction, as long as you know how, and if you want to knock a hole in a specific point of, say, a wall or something solid, you'd use that kind of thing. I'd have a word wiv your boss, mate; you need to go at it from another angle."

So, if the bomb wasn't a terrorist thing, then what the fuck was it? Jacks brain did several sweeps of the surrounding area, and couldn't find anything to land on.

Singer, that fucker. They needed to question him regarding whoever brought in the watch and the necklace: why, why are you robbing dying kids, for fuck's sake? What sort of piece of shit robs two kids in the aftermath of a bomb, and why the fuck just those two and nobody else? The woodpecker was back in full force: peck, peck, peck. He seemed to have bought a farkin' power drill and wasn't letting go.

Albert Singer looked a bit sorry for himself; they'd had his nose put straight, and it looked like it was pretty sore. He had two black eyes nicely developing. Jacks wasn't very sorry; the wanker deserved a slap.

"Now then, son, we can do this shit a couple of ways. I ask the questions and you call for a solicitor, or, I ask the questions, and my lad, Parky, here goes to get a couple of brews and the door is closed, and me and you get familiar. It's all old-fashioned police brutality, son, but before you start crowing, here's the sting, you were found in possession of two items taken from the scene of a terrorist incident, which puts you at the scene. Secondly, if you were at the scene, perhaps you had prior knowledge of the bomb, and that puts you down for 32 counts of murder, and I do believe 46 counts of attempted murder."

"You can't prove any of that!" Singer wasn't having it.

"Alright, son, I have a snitch who puts you there, after the bomb." Jacks was lying through his teeth, but he wanted to turn this fucker and make him sweat.

"Bollocks," Singer retorted, "fucking bollocks!"

Jacks leant back in the chair. "Well, son. I'm not the one looking at thirty-two times life, am I? So, is it bollocks?" He leant forward. Parkinson was smoking a roll-up cigarette, and looking, for all in the world, that this was normal.

Singer was having doubts. "You can't crack me like that; I want a solicitor here and now!"

"Do you now, son? Parky, I do believe it's time for a nice cuppa. And lad, Digestives, I think. They have 'em at the corner shop. Take your time."

Parky stubbed out the cigarette. "Should I close the door on my out, Guv?"

"Yeah, probably best. They'd be a farkin' draught otherwise, and we wouldn't want him catching cold now, eh?"

Singer was sweating; he'd had a beating already, and not being the sharpest tool in the box, the bullshit for the thirty-two count had him a bit rattled. 'The filth' had ways to cook shit up. Parky stood up. Singer went back to representing his name; he grassed up the source of the watch and necklace. He wanted protection, and he wanted it now!

Jacks went directly to call Sofia, couldn't get an answer and asked any patrolling officers to keep an eye out for them. Something made him itch, and it wasn't the fucking woodpecker.

Sofia and Rone had taken some time to go for a walk; they'd headed up around the park and wandered a bit aimlessly past the Serpentine. He'd fancied a pint, but when they got to the door of the pub, he had a bit of what he called 'a moment'. Inside, he was in turmoil. All kinds of images were bouncing around; Sofia lying on the floor, the blood in his mouth, the noise, the shape pulling at his arm…wait, what shape? It was a hidden pocket of a flash of a memory, but something a bit dark and sinister. He did a mental wet dog shake. No, it wasn't real. He had a little shudder.

"You okay?" She asked.

"Yeah, babe…" An hour with Cammie! "Just something a bit odd, dunno, nothing."

There was a patrol car waiting outside the house when they got back. The two officers inside were stepping out as they approached.

"Miss Nyman, Mr Brennan: DI Jacks wants to see you, it's of the utmost urgency."

They looked at each other: what now? Long day, tired, couldn't it wait until tomorrow? No, he was most insistent.

The inside of the patrol car smelled of McDonald's and reminded Rone he was hungry again. The officers walked them through to the office. Sofia was surprised at how messy it was: how did he work like that? He arrived with a mug of tea in one hand and biscuits in the other.

"Thanks for coming." He'd said it as if it was something they could turn down.

"Sofia, your keys, they are just for the house?"

"Yes, of course."

"Were there any other keys on the keyring that fitted anything else?"

"No, just the front door."

He looked a bit more serious than normal and had really bruised knuckles on his right hand. Rone was looking at him with a quizzical look; his internal dialogue was having a game of tennis, and the ball was the questions he wanted to ask.

Had the locks been changed, or were they the same ones?

She looked nervous. "No, nothing changed. What is this about because you're beginning to scare me, and I've been scared enough lately."

Rone was getting a bit riled. "Mate, what the fuck is going on?"

Jacks glanced at him, took a deep breath and picked up the phone. "I need a forensics team to 27 Portland Place, and I want it there ten fucking minutes ago. I don't care, get them back off the missing fucking cat case, and I'll meet them there. You two, stay with me. I don't want you out of my sight until I've made sense of what the bloody hell is going on. We need your fingerprints. I'll have Parky take you down and get that done, then I want to see you both back here. I don't have time to explain, I'll do my best on the way to your house later, Sofia."

They were wiping fingerprint ink off their hands and waiting at Parkinson's side of the messy desk. Sofia noted he was much tidier than his boss, apart from the rolling tobacco that littered the floor. She was holding Rone's hand. He'd gone into a deep silence, and his mind had taken a very long plunge into a very dark place. It rattled around banging off things in the blackness, grasping, but not clinging to anything solid; how could it? At this point, it didn't know what it needed to hang on to.

His nerves were back; they were having a chat with his teeth. He was biting the inside of his lip; he bit so hard he had the taste of blood back in his mouth, and the dark shape leapt up in his mind's eye. "What the fuck is it, what do you want?" He didn't realise he'd said it out loud, and Sofia was looking at him with wide eyes. "Sorry, something is in my head. I can see something, but I can't say what. It's from the night in the pub, it came to me today when we stood at the door to the pub earlier; can't work out where it comes from."

She held his hand a little tighter. "I'm scared, Rone, what's happening?" Her words snapped him back. His mind did a priorities reshuffle, and he reached over to pull her close.

"We'll work it out. Look at me." Sofia leant out of the hug, and she caught the look on his face; it was the most serious she'd ever seen him.

"Nothing and nobody will ever hurt you again. I don't care who it is, or what it is, trust me, they have to kill me first."

The name that Singer had given them was Grimaldi, Franco Grimaldi. He'd been the cellmate of Singer in Pentonville prison. He was a malicious nasty fucker. He was known to have connections in a bigger group of the London-based Mafia; he'd do anything for them that involved violence, and generally making a mess of people. He had a file an inch thick, and he had a 'thing' for violence against women, especially young women. He'd bragged to Singer about spending time watching them, and 'getting into their homes', as he'd said. He was a nasty violent fucker. Hence Singer being shit scared of the consequences of spilling his name.

Jacks had called a meeting with his top boss, somehow.

He said, "We're looking at two different crimes here. First, the bombing; the explosives 'bods' don't reckon it was a terror bomb, their report would be on his desk first thing tomorrow. Secondly, the two kids, Nyman and Brennan, had been targeted for their possessions, and the things taken from them had turned up in a pawn shop run by a known wrong'un, Albert Singer. Now, Singer had connections with an Italian 'mob ride along' called Grimaldi, and he'd been stupid enough to sell the kids' chain and watch to Singer. Now, they wanted to know why Grimaldi targeted just Rone and Sofia. He had forensics at the house because they suspected Grimaldi had the keys he'd taken from the girl's coat."

Top boss looked up. "Good work. I'll get on the phone to Mc Nee, brief him and call another meeting of the heads of department. Let me see what the report says, this lot just took a turn. Well done, Jacks, let me know if you find anything at the house."

Jacks was with Sofia and Rone on the way to Portland Place. Parky rode shotgun, and they were in the back of the bloody awful Cortina.

"Sofia, who else had access to the house?" Jacks asked.

"My dad obviously, and Betty the lady who cleans a couple of times a week, normally on a Monday and a Thursday."

"Betty?"

"Dodds, Mrs Dodds." She'd known her pretty much all her life, lovely lady.

Did she know where she lived? Of course, she had a flat not so far from Portland Place. Good, he'd send someone around to get her prints. Parky noted the address.

"Now, what's happening here?" Rone asked.

Jacks pursed his lips and took a breath as his brain fired up and pulled bits of info from its own chaos.

"We found your watch, Rone, and Sofia's chain in a pawn shop. We believe someone took them from you when you were unconscious after the explosion." He didn't want to add they were the only ones robbed. "The person who took them is known to us; he's quite an unpleasant sort of bloke, and we have reason to believe he's been into your house, Sofia. The forensics team are searching the place now."

But why? Rone had all this getting banged off the walls in his head. Who was this dickhead? What did he want? The questions came pouring out: why, what for, and why a few more times, just for good measure. Sofia had gone very quiet, and he didn't like that at all.

The road was full of police cars and vans; figures moved around inside the house with white disposable overalls on. Jacks spotted a familiar face: Alisha Gupta. She headed up the team inside, and she'd found a few things she wanted him to see.

She looked at Rone and Sofia. "You sure you want them to hear this?" She asked Jacks.

He did because he needed Sofia to check some things in her room, and this shit bag was a trophy collector. So yeah, let's hear what she had.

"Well, he's a clumsy bugger, and for a known 'crim', he'd been pretty careless with touching some things."

Jacks had a feeling he knew what, but waited. Alisha led them upstairs to Sofia's room. There was fingerprint dust on the furniture. Opposite her bed was a dresser with three drawers; it was normally white, but at the moment it was covered in silver dust.

"So we can eliminate certain prints in the room," she looked at Rone in particular, "Miss Nyman and Mr Brennan, but he appears to have left a print on the inside of this draw. He was careless here."

"Which draw?" Sofia asked.

Alisha took a breath. "The draw that contains your underwear, Miss Nyman."

The moment swirled around the room several times, rushed in and hit Sofia square in the chest. She didn't expect it to hit so hard.

"Oh my god, why?"

Alisha made a small movement with her head, shaking it back and forth. "Not sure, but as horrible as this sounds, can we ask you to see if there is anything missing?"

She opened the drawer. "We removed the things, but the team has replaced them exactly as they were." She didn't want to say at this point that they'd photographed her underwear.

Rone looked shocked. "You mean he's been in the room, in the house, poking around?"

Alisha nodded. "I would certainly say so, Mr Brennan."

Rone shook his head again. The vision was back, mocking him, taunting from the dark corner of his mind. "Fucker," he muttered, "fucker indeed."

Alisha said, "Sorry, Miss. Can I ask you to check, please?"

Jacks felt it appropriate to step back, and Alisha placed a hand in the middle of Sofia's back; she made a small circular motion. It was a subconscious act of one woman comforting another whose space had been violated. Alisha had seen this kind of thing before.

Sofia was looking at her panties and bras; her eyes widened. "Okay." She shook a little and lifted each pair out of the draw. Mrs Dodds did the laundry, and she had a way of folding her pants, left side over the right. It was a 'thing'; she'd always done it, and some of these were mixed up, right over left.

"Did any of the team unfold these?" She asked.

"No, everything was removed as it was; each item." Her hands were shaking a little as she went through the items.

"There are some missing," she said.

Alisha continued the small circular motion and looked at Rone and Jacks. "Boys, can you give us a moment, please?"

Rone gulped air. His system wasn't accepting the reality at the moment, and it wanted a sit-down and have a cuppa tea, with a lot of sugar. Jacks guided him to the door. "C'mon, son, this way, let's go and have a chat."

"Can you tell me which of your underwear is missing, Miss Nyman?"

"Sofia, please," she said. Sofia took a moment to compose herself. "I had some lace panties. There were three pairs, white, French lace." They'd been a gift from her mother; for whatever reason, her mum thought she could do with some 'nice knickers' as she'd put it. But they were not there. She blushed. She'd worn a pair of them for Rone. Her face reddened, and Alisha nodded and closed her eyes for a brief moment. Hmmm…The ones she had worn for Rone, when had this been? A couple of days ago. She blushed a little again. And where would they be now? Sofia took a beat; she'd put them in the wash basket.

She eyed the wicker basket in the corner of the room. Alisha pulled on a pair of latex gloves and lifted the lid. Very carefully she took out the items inside; some of Rone's things, mostly Sofia's. No French lace underwear. He'd been in the house in the last two days and had taken them. The gravity of the moment did several laps around the inside of her mind. Things were coming at her way too fast, and she couldn't control any of the emotions charging and banging their way around inside her head. She felt tears trickle down her face.

Alisha stood motionless in front of her. "I'm sorry, Sofia." Was there anything else missing? She didn't think so.

"You've been very strong; that was a very courageous thing to do, thank you."

Alisha briefed Jacks; it was very incredibly serious. "We need to secure the house, and we need to go through every room with a fine tooth comb if we're gonna get the bastard. We need to do it right."

Jacks nodded. "Those kids can't stay here, can they?"

She shook her head. "Speaking as a woman, I'd say she's feeling beyond vulnerable right now. I don't think they could stay here. I wouldn't."

Jacks' agreed. He had to put them somewhere. Wasn't there an aunt? Or a hotel for a couple of nights. And where the fuck was her father?

"Can I ask you two to gather some things, enough for a couple of nights away? We need to find you somewhere to stay. The team will finish up here in the next few days, and we can't have you here."

Sofia went to her room. Alisha was there taking photos of possible marks on the floor.

"Can I take some things, please?"

"Of course, let me help."

She took a small backpack and went through the wardrobe to find tops, some jeans and socks. She avoided the draw with her underwear. In the bathroom, she found her toothbrush and packed a wash bag with some make-up. Everything felt soiled and dirty, she didn't want to touch any of it. The shops had long since closed or she would have gone to buy everything new. Rone busied around and threw things in his carrier bags. He'd not got around to getting any kind of bag yet, and the Co-op ones were doing okay.

Where to put them: this was the question. Jacks was wracking his head. The aunt wasn't any good, she was as mad as a box of frogs. The father's cousin Paul, but they couldn't get an answer from his phone numbers. Time was getting on. It was massively unconventional, but he had no choice.

"Is it okay to use this phone?"

The white overall nodded.

"Hello, love, it's me. Can you make up the spare room? We have a couple of guests coming. Yeah, be about an hour."

Chapter 12
Mummy

Jacks lived up in Finchley, Sheldon Avenue, the three-bedroom house set back from the road. The kids had been quiet on the ride up from Portland Place. Jacks hummed quietly to himself as they weaved their way through the evening traffic. London drifted past the window, and Rone watched as the lights and city passed. Sofia sat staring out the front of the car; her thoughts were a mix of 'whys' and 'why me'…She felt empty and drained, tired again, and she glanced across at Rone as he looked vacantly out the window.

She did a double breath in; he looked pale and thinner, more worried than she'd ever seen him. They'd only known each other a few months, but she felt that she'd known him all her life. "Rone." He looked back. The blue eyes attached some Scuba kit and went for a look.

She took his hand. "You can go anytime you want, you know, you shouldn't stay if you don't want to."

He looked square back at her. "I can't go anywhere." He placed his hand flat on her chest, pressing slightly between and above her breasts. He was looking back and trying not to blink. "How can I go anywhere? My heart is beating next to yours, I can feel it; if I go anywhere without you, I'm scared it will just stop. You're the single reason I'm still alive. I saw you that night; I saw you and knew that I had to get back for you. There's a reason I'm here: you're *it*."

Jacks had been trying not to listen. He could be a jaded fucker and at 46 he'd heard most things, but that…fuck me, that boy is a bit of a diamond, needs a polish-like, but he reminds me of his dad: fired clip after clip that night in Korea. Jacks had bombed the clips as fast as his shaking hands could press the rounds in, but Harry kept firing, rallied the boys, "Pick 'em off at a distance, don't let them get close or we're fucked and we'll get overrun. Keep the rate of fire up lads, rate of fire." Chug chug chug, the rate of fire of the Bren gun slow and steady, but Harry was not letting up.

Irene Jacks was busy in the kitchen when they arrived; he'd let them in through the front door. "Shoes off, please." Mrs Jacks was a bit particular. Irene came out of the kitchen, a warm smile on her face; she was small, only about 5 feet, dressed in an apron, a pleated skirt and a blue blouse, with her brown shoulder-length hair perfectly in place.

"C'mon in, that's it, through to the lounge." The lounge had been knocked through to make a large living space; dining table with four chairs, three piece suite, all very tasteful. They stood slightly awkwardly in the middle of the room.

"Come along, dear, show them to their room; they can freshen up. Dinner is almost ready." She'd wondered what they would eat and had settled on making shepherd's pie, and a nice apple crumble for dessert. Rone thought the house smelled amazing, just like his nan's. He was starving as normal.

Jacks showed them upstairs. At the top, the hallway led off to the bathroom and three bedrooms. "You're in here." He opened the door and smiled to see Irene had made up two beds. "Look, I may be an old fart, but I understand you need each other right now; so, here we are, sort yourselves out and come down when you're ready."

Rone wolfed down three helpings of shepherd's pie and barely looked up while he was doing it. It made Sofia smile inside and out; he always ate like someone was going to steal his food. The house was warm and she'd finished eating. Irene had begun washing up; they sat on the sofa, no TV on in the house, Radio 4 burbled away in the background.

Jacks came and sat opposite. "Sorry, you two, I need to talk shop for a moment. Sofia, where is your father? We have no contact details for him; we tried his company but they were not cooperating. We need to tell him about the house and ask him some questions regarding the contents of his safe."

"He's normally in Bern or Zurich; he's on business and he usually calls once or twice a week, but this last week he'd not done so."

"Any reason for that?" Jacks asked.

No, it was his way. Were they close? She shrugged. "When things are going well for me, he's there." He had arranged agents, driven her to castings and provided a fund for her to draw on. She didn't want for anything.

He smiled back at her. "You avoided my question, Sofia."

She looked at the floor, back at Jacks. "No, I don't suppose we are, really. He was absent. I grew up looking after myself, boarded at drama school in Kent, came home on odd weekends and stayed with friends. Mummy left for work in New York, so performing became my family, and now I can't perform because someone blew me up and stole my things, and broke into my house and stole more of my things!" Tears rolled down her cheeks. Rone was biting his lip.

Jacks pushed on. "Your dad, he's something in insurance, something to do with underwriting insurance for large corporates, is that correct? So money shouldn't be an issue."

"No," she snapped the word back.

Then why, Jacks asked himself, was the London mob sending animals to rob his daughter and scare the shit out of her? Why indeed!

Rone had spotted a photo on the mantelpiece, amongst photos of Irene, various family etc. A group of soldiers was gathered around the front of a crashed American fighter plane in a semi-circle, some taking a knee, others standing behind.

"Can I?" He looked back at Jacks.

"Ah yeah, of course, son." He sat back down, trying to pick out Jacks.

Sofia looked up at Rone and looked back at the picture. "The lad in the middle, is that you, Rone?"

She laughed. "You're a time traveller, you're Dr Who! What are you doing in the army?"

Jacks smiled back. "Ah yeah, that's your dad, Rone. Me and him served in Korea together."

"Korea?" Rone knew his dad had been in the forces, but he never really spoke of it.

"No, he wouldn't, son; bet he never told you he was Harry Brennan MM either?"

"MM?"

"Military medal son; your dad is a bit of a hero boy. See that plane and the pilot? That's where your watch came from. He saved a lot of lives on Gloucester Hill." His mind wandered off. The noise, flashes, screams, the battle noise raged in his head when it wanted to, nothing he could do about that, just get on. Time had passed.

"C'mon, you two, if you want a bath, there's plenty of hot water. Early start tomorrow, so up you go."

When he'd said it, he didn't really mean for them to have a bath together, but...never mind!

"I still think it's you in the photo."

They'd pushed the beds together and were snuggled under the covers. Everything smelled fresh and clean, of soap, and reminded Rone of home. For the first time, he wandered off and missed his mum and dad. "I had no idea about my dad, and imagine him and Jacks having been in a war together. I mean, bloody hell, you'd never think looking at him that he had been in a war."

Carl Nyman was in Zurich, but more than that, he was in trouble. The meeting with the clients had not gone well. He'd not managed to secure the guarantees for some of the properties and they wanted to know why. He'd call the office in the morning and get them to fax the copies and the details. Doing business in Switzerland was never simple.

Firstly, the Swiss and their infuriating habit of wanting to dissect every piece of information; then the client was Italian, so another cultural divide. The Italians had been silent during the first meeting, more animated in the second, and now the air positively crackled with tension. Carl's brain was buzzing at a thousand miles per hour, and his normal calm exterior had run to the bathroom for a piss. He was starting to flap.

Matteo Farina motioned to the Swiss representatives to leave and folded his fingers together. "Mr Nyman, you do understand we've funded you for some time; the payments on the house, the lifestyle and your position in your company are valuable to us. But, we do need our investment to be returned. We do not appreciate having to wait for you to ensure that this is done and done correctly and on time. The land in London is going to be built on."

The property there now was of little value, but if they appeared to be investing in the regeneration of poor areas of London, then they needed to be able to move quickly, the buildings insured, then damaged beyond repair, the insurance policies paid out and the permission to build approved.

Carl understood, but he had to cover his tracks; then surely Matteo understood? He didn't. They had bought and paid for their man, and he didn't want excuses. Had Carl not received his message a few weeks ago? Their patience was wearing thin then; it was almost worn out now. Perhaps more action was needed. Carl took a moment and looked at Farina with shock, the colour drained from his face; it had somewhere else to be, not in the room with whatever was happening here.

"Message?" He asked.

Farina would not elaborate further.

"The bomb? You blew up a pub and almost killed my child? That was you?"

Farina took a slow breath in. "No, Carl, we would do nothing so obvious. Maybe you should think about the events after; the media coverage, for example, and maybe ask Sofia, such a wonderful name, beautiful girl, where her keys and jewellery are. And the boy, now, he was a surprise, surely below her level, Carl no? Did they find his watch?"

Carl knew nothing of these events. He'd not spoken to Sofia about it and had no idea of watches, keys or jewellery. What were they talking about? The paperwork was a glitch;

he'd get it solved, but Sofia…what keys, what message? His composure ran around the room in its underpants, and they were not very clean. Back in the hotel, he'd dialled home. The phone rang three maybe four times, and a strange woman's voice with a slight Indian accent answered. Did he dial the wrong number? "And who the hell are you, and what are you doing in my house?"

Alisha took a moment. "Is that Mr Nyman? I'm Alisha Gupta. I'm with the Met. There has been an incident at your home. Where are you at the moment?"

Panic flooded in. His composure was drowning now in the same messy underpants.

No, she couldn't talk on the phone, when was he back? No, his daughter was safe. Again, she couldn't say where, but he should know that she wasn't harmed.

Again, "When are you back?"

"Day after tomorrow."

Really, no sense of urgency to get back to his daughter?

He couldn't leave. If he did, then he would lose everything, Alisha was not one to judge, but she thought he was doing that anyway. He spoke again. She struggled to hear; there was a hiss on the phone, two or three clicks in rapid succession. It cleared.

"Sorry, Mr Nyman, can you repeat please?"

"I'll be home in two days."

Where was his daughter now? Alisha didn't know, and in the back of her mind, something did its own clicking and making whir noises. She'd heard that before somewhere.

Carl was flapping so hard he could have taken flight! What the fuck was happening? He tried to call Farina to set up another meeting. He was waiting for the documents via fax in the morning. Until then, he was going to have to try to calm down, but calm was out for a jog in the evening air, and he went to the minibar instead. If calm wasn't playing, he'd make it play along at some point.

Alisha was in Jacks office when he arrived, talking with Parky. They had processed the house and found nothing more. The evidence they had found was in the safe in the evidence room.

"How did you open the safe at the house?" He asked.

"Simple really. Most blokes are pretty stupid, but even this wanker couldn't forget his daughter's birthday. 150362, simple."

She cracked a smile and cracked a safe by all accounts. Clever lady, Alisha Gupta.

Jacks nodded. "Good work."

"Thanks."

"Cuppa tea?"

"Yes."

"Okay, take a seat."

Parky at this point knew he was a tea boy; how would she like it?

"Milk, and two please, nice and sweet, just like me!"

Parky laughed. "Yeah, right, I work with you; there ain't a sweet bone in your body, lady."

Alisha eyed Jacks. "The phone is bugged."

"What? Okay, this gets deeper and deeper. Can we find out by who?"

"I'm not sure. I've asked a mate at…oh what's it called now…British Telecom to see if they can pin it down. She wasn't hopeful, but it was an old-school tap; normally you can't hear them, but if someone is dumb enough to hang up, or pick up, it causes the line to make some noises. I heard it last night. Nyman called, he's in Switzerland on business; won't or can't come back. He wanted to know where she was."

Jacks attention snapped to attention. "You didn't tell him, eh?"

No, she wasn't as daft as he looked! Parky arrived with tea.

"Ohhh," she cooed, "good little lad you are."

Parky tutted. "I expect you want a roll-up as well?"

Her brown eyes flashed a smile. "You get better all the time."

Carl had drunk his composure into submission; it was tired after its run, and by the time he finished the minibar, it couldn't run anymore. The following morning, 'composure' had a bitch of a hangover. He had to get straight and convince Farina that everything was in place. He showered, dressed, and would have liked breakfast, but his hangover and rotating stomach bypassed the option. He had coffee while he waited for London to get to the office. He called his secretary three or four times; where was she, silly girl? Finally, she answered; he needed copies of the agreements for Canary Wharf and he needed them faxed to this number. He asked her to read it back, double-checked she had the number correct, and hung up. Next, he tried the house again. Nothing, no answer: whatever is going on, it would have to wait.

By the time he got to the Swiss office, the fax had arrived. The Swiss were pouring over the details, and Farina and the Italians were in a huddle. Farina smoked French Gauloises cigarettes, and they smelled incredibly strong. The smell rushed in, and gave Carl's hangover a smack around the back of the head: it was in no place to fight back and just accepted the slap.

"All seems to be in order, Mr Nyman."

They turned to Farina, and the other 'suits'; they could agree to terms.

The hangover sat back and took a moment to clear a little. Carl stayed put, the Swiss left and the other suits made themselves scarce.

Farina pulled another Gaulioses out of the packet, lit up and relaxed back into the chair. "We hear there was a 'disturbance' at your house, and your daughter is missing."

How could he possibly know that?

"Ways and means, Carl, ways and means. Where is she?"

He didn't know, and why would Farina want to know now? The deal is as good as done.

Farina reached into his pocket pulled out some French lace panties and dropped them on the table. "I can only imagine how pretty she looks in these." Would he like to know where they came from?

Carl felt the taste of bile in his mouth. He was about to lose the battle with the hangover, and he vomited on the carpet.

Farina looked on with distaste. "Dignity, Carl. You seem to have lost it on the carpet. Now, go back to London and make sure everything goes as it should. Or we will find her, and you *will* understand."

Concorde took just under three hours to fly from New York to London. Jackie Nyman sat back and watched the Mach meter click to Mach 2; such a thrill travelling faster than a bullet. Two and a half hours later, the beautiful delta-winged aircraft turned onto the finals and roared over the fence into Heathrow. The normal crowd of plane spotters 'oooohed' and 'aaaaghed.' Camera shutters clicked. 'Speedbird Concorde One' was taxiing to its specific air bridge. Jackie was back in the UK. She hated London and felt it drab and dreary after New York. She hated it almost as much as she hated being called Mrs Nyman.

She'd tried the house number several times to reach Sofia. They'd only spoken once since the dreadful bomb; poor girl, she did sound out of sorts, but she always had her theatre friends and the new production. Jackie was, as usual, out of touch with what was happening with Sofia. She breezed through customs and had a porter gather her bags. A car from the publishing company was waiting. She had appointments; the great thing with Concorde was arriving before you left!

She met with clients. The office overlooked the post office tower. She'd fancied lunch in the restaurant, but apparently, it was closed because, ironically, of bomb threats. Did they close all the pubs and cinemas in London because of some awful threat? She didn't think so. Ridiculous.

She'd phoned the house several times, but no reply. Where was Sofia? She wanted to see her. She called her friend Rachel.

"No, Mrs Nyman, she's not in the production. She'd become very unwell and the understudy had taken the role."

Had Rachel heard from her recently? No, she'd been busy and had not. She did try to keep in touch. Dreadful girl. Jackie span up, her brain racing now, flicked through the pages of her Filofax. There, Mrs Dodds. She dialled the number; Betty answered.

"Hello, yes?"

"Mrs Dodds, it's Jackie."

Betty almost snapped to attention. "Yes, hello, Jackie dear, what can I do for you?"

"Have you seen or heard from Sofia?"

Betty ran the information through her cleaning lady circuit board. "Well, my dear, there's been an awful kerfuffle at the house, police everywhere. They came and took my fingers you know?"

"Took your fingers, Betty?"

"Prints, my fingers' prints." She spoke in plurals.

This was just awful. Where was her useless ex-husband? No doubt shagging that poor girl he kept on a string at his office. She called the office. No, he was away, not back until late today or possibly tomorrow. Jackie was reaching the end of her very short fuse, which was connected to her explosive temper, and it was in danger of her going bang, and reducing a number of people to ashes.

She called for the car. "Take me to Portland Place. I'll find her, someone must know what is going on." There was a police car parked outside the house. The black BMW 7 series parked behind it, and she went to knock on the window. The officer inside jumped and wound down the window. He was confronted by a tall blonde woman who looked very wound up. "Yes, madam, how may I help?"

"What is going on here?" She demanded, "And where is my daughter?"

"The house is closed up madam."

She could see that her powers of observation were not absent. "What had happened here? Again, please give me an answer and not a statement!"

"DI Jacks, madam, you'd need to speak to him. I have his number or you can find him at the station."

"Which station?"

"Broadway, madam."

Did she know where it was?

Her driver knew. She was in the reception area causing carnage when Jacks walked down from his office.

"Mrs Nyman?"

"Yes, don't call me that, and who are you?"

"Worried," he thought to himself, "that would be my middle name right now!"

"If you'd like to come through this way." He was wondering at this point how the girl got to be as nice as she was; the father was absent and the mum an absolute bitch. It's going to be a long day. "Please take a seat." Jackie flapped at the chair and sat down.

"Where, may I ask, is she?"

"She's in a close protection unit at the moment." She was actually drinking coffee on his sofa watching TV with Rone, but the fewer people knew that the better.

Parky hovered. "Would you like some tea at all?"

No, she wanted her daughter. She couldn't calm down; her system was booted for trouble, and it was going to make it, no matter what.

It took Jacks just over an hour to fill her in on the details, in which time her system had decided to take a pill and have a little snooze.

"Okay," she said, "I understand. So at this point, detective inspector, what can I do?"

Good point; what could she do? "They need a safe spot to stay. I mean they are safe now, but it's very short term."

"For how long?"

"Well, until some of this unravels, Jackie." He'd received several severe looks for 'Mrs Nyman'.

Who was this boy, and where did he come from? He talked her through the story of Rone and Sofia. "He sounds charming," the hint of sarcasm not lost.

"He's actually a really nice lad, I know his father quite well."

"Really?" Jackie was surprised. "Was he a criminal?"

"No," Jacks said, "he'd been a very courageous soldier."

Jackie nodded approval. "Okay, I need to take charge here. They should come to New York."

"No, Jackie, it's not an option. I need them here fairly close. The threat to them is still at large, and I need to be able to talk to them, and I can't do it if they are in the United States. They are part of the ongoing investigation."

"What about the boy's family? If they don't know anything about him, hide them in plain sight, dear inspector."

He was 'dear inspector' now, things were improving. But it was 50% of an idea, could she bear with him? She sat back and surveyed the chaos that was Jacks desk: my goodness, how did he do it?

Chapter 13
Grimaldi

Grimaldi had seen the police car waiting for Rone and Sofia; he'd parked further along Portland Place so he could watch the house. He'd seen them leave earlier in the day and was tempted to go back in again, just so he could take his time. He'd enjoyed going through the draw, liked to smell her perfumes, touch the clothes in the wardrobe. He'd spent some time there, but he didn't need to get caught in the house; he'd wait and bide his time. He saw them leave with the officers in the car. They'd looked annoyed at having to go. Now was his chance to go in; he knew he'd have at least an hour, but maybe he'd hang on, just in case. He sat back in the seat and twirled the fabric in his pocket.

Twenty minutes later, a white Ford Transit van and two patrol cars arrived. Alisha Gupta and her team had taken keys from Sofia for the house. Grimaldi sank lower in his seat. He could glimpse what was going on through the gap between the steering wheel and the dash. "What do we have here? Now what the fuck is this?" The team were pulling on overalls and letting themselves in. Grimaldi thought it was time to leave. He'd let them get inside and then he'd reverse out, so he didn't need to pass them.

Thinking back, he'd quite enjoyed the last time he'd put his hands on her. It was quite unexpected; he was going to rob them in the street, make it look like a mugging. He'd been waiting in the car outside the pub, he'd pretty much followed her all day. And when she met the boy, well, 'double the fun': he'd planned on stabbing the boy, just the once to make him bleed, but her…he was going to take a bit of time and get a bit rough. He'd have liked that: "Just make sure she was fucked up enough to send the right message to Carl Nyman. He'd had a big pay-out, and been slow to react on demands," they'd said. But the explosion; he didn't have *that* on the cards.

He knew he had to act fast after the place blew. The windows were gone, the door hanging off; he could look like a citizen trying to help. They wanted the keys to the Nyman's place, make things easier in the future to gain access to Nyman when the time came. And having followed her around, *he* wanted the keys to the place. Pretty little thing, she was.

The pub was smoke and chaos inside, and he hadn't seen her at first. He almost stepped on the boy; he was lying on his back between two blokes, with a lump of the bar lying on his arm. He was bleeding out the side of his chest; ah, shame, he looked like he was dead to Grimaldi. He saw the watch; nice, why not, I'll have that. Now, where is Nyman's daughter? She lay on the floor, half under a bloke's legs, her bag caught in her hand. He'd gone into the bag to look for the keys; nothing. So, maybe her coat pocket. Her coat was half off, only on one arm, so he'd pulled it off, and once he'd found the keys, he threw the coat in the corner.

He stepped back to the girl, her eyes closed, her breathing spasmodic; she was covered in white dust, looked for all the world like a little dolly. She was wearing a chain with a star on it: he'd have that. He popped the clasp and dropped it in his pocket with the keys. By this time, 'good citizens' were arriving, so he'd pretended to be helping, and then left.

But the bomb was not the only strange occurrence that night. Just before the place blew, he'd seen a face he knew, and with the face, a bloke carrying a sports bag. They were talking; the 'face' had held the door open for a couple of Nyman's daughter's friends who were leaving. They'd been in the restaurant together; the little thing with the curls looked a bit pissed, and matey boy was helping her along. He'd wait. Now, where had he seen that face before? He'd have to have a think; close to closing up time, better get into the game. The bag man walked out without the bag; he'd left it with the face. Something happening there…hmmm…the face, the face? Boom, the explosion. Time for a plan B.

Once he worked out, the police were getting more sniffy, he put things together. He'd go and see Singer, get the watch and chain back. He was a bit of a useless fucker, and Grimaldi didn't need him spilling his guts when and if the plod knocked. He'd backed out of the street and headed directly to the pawn shop. He parked a few hundred yards from the place and walked a roundabout way to get to it. The front door was boarded up, and he could tell the place had been raided. Fuck, fucking Singer, fuck! He'd deal with that fucker later; he needed to get off the street, get in touch with 'them' and have a think.

If 'the filth' had got Singer, and they'd taken the two kids, what to do? His head was turning over little snippets and flashes of cutting Singer's balls off and watching the fucker choke on them when he rammed them down his throat, fucking piece of shit. Nyman's daughter and the boy were a fucking luxury item right now, he had to get organised.

He'd talked to his contact. They'd given him an address to stay at, they'd dispose of the car, leave it in the car park behind the Green Man pub. There would be a silver Vauxhall Viva, the keys under the mat, the door would be open, call in a couple of days, stay low. Nyman would be back, and they were beginning to think he'd outlived his purpose. It may be time to have him dealt with, just so others in the organisation know that it was a serious game. They'd do the daughter as well; best not leave anything to chance. Grimaldi was looking forward to that part.

'Top boss' had called Jacks up to the office. He was just back from a meeting with Mc Nee and the other heads of departments. Once he'd presented the report on the bomb, with the evidence from the explosives guys, it did seem clear enough this was not a terror bombing. The counter-terrorist units had stood down at that point, they had enough going on. The Home Secretary had agreed with the findings, but having taken advice from, Mc Nee, he would let the 'terrorist' aspect keep hanging; no need to let whoever had placed the device know they were looking elsewhere.

How were the children?

"Children?" Jacks looked at him with a large question mark in the middle of his face. "Children, boss?"

"The Nyman girl, and the lad, Brennan. Wasn't that his name?"

"Yes, safe enough for now boss. We're planning to move them as soon as we get things arranged."

"The character that's after them, nasty piece of work isn't he?" The boss asked.

Nasty. Jacks ideas of nasty did a quick check of the nasty scale, and Grimaldi had written the fucking scale. "Nasty enough, boss, yes, a real piece of work."

"Gupta tells me the phone at the Nyman house is bugged," the boss added.

"Tapped is the term," Jacks corrected, "yes, we reckon it is."

"Can we get the 'spooks' on that, see where the tap is directed from?" Top boss asked.

"I think Alisha has made contact with someone inside the phone company, but wouldn't be a bad thing if we could get MI5 to have a poke around to see. Any help is appreciated."

"Okay, I'll make some calls. Thanks, Jacks, keep me updated."

Jacks headed out, the sarcasm filter in his head was always blocked when talking to the top boss. 'Keep me updated'. *I was thinking of going to the pub and getting pissed, boss,* Jacks thought, *but 'updated' comes in close.*

Now he had to deal with Jackie Nyman again; the idea of getting Sofia and Rone out of the way and out of London wasn't half bad. He'd sent her to the house; it was high time someone from her family was present, and anything to get her out of the station and away from him. She made him nervous, in a way storming Chinese infantry had some years ago! He had some calls to make to see if he could make arrangements.

He was waiting for Harry to call back; half a plan was in his head to get Rone and Sofia close to Harry's place. Didn't his dad have a farm, or work on a farm, or some shit with farms? Wasn't Rone born in a cowshed or somewhere daft,

Harry had said the other week when they'd met? Something to do wiv farms.

Jackie was on her way to Finchley. She'd cancelled appointments for the rest of the day, and she'd taken the car and driver. With the mood she was in, nobody was going to ask questions; she was fierce when in action, they'd all had a mental assault at some point. But they all knew the story behind the bombing and Sofia. The surprising part was seeing Jackie so emotional about her daughter. Normally, it was a quick lunch, meetings, possibly a dinner and Concorde back to New York.

The driver was new. She sat in the back of the BMW looking at the back of his head. She'd not seen him before: he was like all the drivers from the company they used, smart and well-presented. He was, she thought, of a pleasant demeanour, spoke when he was spoken to, had extremely good posture, was not like the normal drivers with a bit of a paunch and carried himself well.

"What is your name, young man?" She asked.

"Paul, madam."

"Please don't call me madam, makes me sound like someone who runs a brothel. Call me Jackie, never call me Mrs Nyman, and we'll get along just fine. Do you know where you're going, Paul?"

"The address was clear, Jackie, thank you. I looked it up on the A to Z."

"You know you're mine for the rest of the day, and for as long as I need you in the next possible few days? I don't want to change drivers, I don't like it. Is that understood?"

"Very good, Jackie, not a problem for me."

Paul took a long look in the mirror. She was looking at some notes in her hand, head down; he put her about forty-ish, strong features, her blond hair quite short. She was quite tall, possibly five feet ten, slim; she was very well dressed, trouser suit, for business obviously. Stern lady, but he reckoned she had a bit of a soft side, but just a thought.

He did a double look in the rearview mirror. There was a blue Ford Capri that had turned a couple of times when they had. His attention notched up a gear, and he looked for telltale signs that would give the car away; sticker in the window, shit dangling from the mirror…no, nothing. He made a right turn, slowed, and waited for the Capri to follow. It did. He drove on for about one hundred yards, checked the mirror and turned again. The Capri sailed past. He made another right and was back on the Finchley Road.

"Everything okay, Paul?" She asked.

"Yes, Jackie, all good. Just a precaution."

Precaution to what, she wondered.

Jacks had called Irene and told her that Jackie was on the way. "Put your iron pants on, love, she's a bit of a fire-breathing dragon. I wouldn't wanna be in young Rone's shoes when she gets there! She's going to take them to get clothes; they can't go back to the house, and they need things to wear. I've put two of the boys on the car she's in, she won't know they are there."

Paul had already seen them.

The BMW parked on the road. Paul was out to get the door for Jackie.

"Will you stay with the car, Paul?"

"Yes, I'll be just here." He'd say she marched to the door and knocked like the police!

He stepped back around the front of the BMW, pretending to look at the grill. He was looking at the blue Ford Capri that had parked about five cars down. "Now, mate, who the fuck might you boys be then?"

Sofia had seen the car arrive, then saw as her mother emerged. Yes, that was the word she'd use; she thought she looked like the alien in the film, when it rears up above Ripley.

"Rone, my mother is here."

He did a big swallow of tea, and his nerves jumped up to say hello. Could they move in for a while and get comfortable? This next bit was gonna be worth watching.

Irene got the door. "Oh, Mrs Nyman, so nice to meet you!"

Jackie winced at the name.

"Come in, dear, they are in the lounge. Would you mind popping your shoes off?"

Jackie almost recoiled. "Shoes?"

"Yes, dear. House rule, no shoes inside, dear."

It was more a reaction than an action, but Jackie slipped her shoes off and left them on the mat. "Tea, dear?"

She shook her head. "No, thank you."

Sofia was in the doorway to the lounge. "Mummy!"

Jackie took a moment. "Sofia, darling! I'm so sorry, all this has been dreadful!"

Sofia thought 'dreadful' a slight understatement, but then her mother was not one to exaggerate.

She reached out, pulled Sofia in, held her very tight, and left 'uptight' Jackie to take a rest.

"Now, Inspector Jacks tells me I have an hour or so. I have the car here, and he's arranging somewhere for you to go and stay away from London. I wanted you in New York, but apparently, that is not going to happen."

Rone was standing. He was back to biting his lip; any harder and he'd eat his face from the inside out.

"Come through, Mummy, I want you to meet Rone."

She stepped into the lounge and Rone stood in front of the sofa. Jackie took a moment. He was a skinny kid, with kind brown eyes; his smile was honest, but his expression was struggling to keep it all in place. He also had a withered-looking left arm and a nasty scar, a short flat-top haircut, was wearing jeans, a crumpled t-shirt and his socks needed changing. Sofia had warned him not to call her Mrs Nyman. His hands did a pointless little motion as if to reach to shake her hand, but doubt was sitting with his nerves and having fun.

For all her abrupt manner, Jackie knew when to tone things down. Jacks had explained a lot about Rone. He'd told her how he'd almost died in the bombing, how Sofia had spent so much time with him, the fact they were just kids was not, he thought, an issue. He'd seen victims of trauma on enough occasions, and he felt at this time they needed each other. If the relationship was to burn itself out, then it would, but he had a great deal of respect for young Rone. He'd been through a lot, as had Sofia.

"So please, I don't know you from Adam, but I'd ask that you take it a little easy on them." He could have a voice of authority when he wanted.

Jackie had soaked up the words, filed them under 'action noted', and she reached out her hand. "Rone, darling boy, I've heard so much about you."

Rone almost passed out; he swore the room did a full loop!

"Now," she motioned to the car outside, "we have an hour or so. Irene, where are the nearest shops of some value?" Irene thought Brent Cross probably fitted the bill.

"Perfect. Okay, guys," she'd suddenly slipped into Americanisms, "shall we go?"

Rone's nerves had become quite bored and left via the back door.

"Could I sit in the front, please, Jackie?" She shot a glance at Paul.

"Fine, Jackie, no problem." He reached out his hand to Rone. "I'm Paul. Jump in, fella."

Rone thought the BMW was a bit of a spaceship inside. It purred and felt really smooth. They glided through the traffic, and it made the Cortina feel like the shit box it was. He had a little chuckle to himself: 'shit box'.

Paul had his radar looping for the Capri, and sure enough there it was. If it was a tail they were shit at it. He stayed at the limit, no point in trying to lose them, and when they arrived at Brent Cross he parked in the upper-level car park. He'd nosey parked the BMW, and watched in the rearview mirror for the Capri. He didn't see it; they perhaps parked on the level down to wait for them to leave. Paul was a thorough sort of lad, and although he didn't want to speak out of place, he'd have to ask.

"Jackie, can I have a word, please?" He glanced at Rone and Sofia.

She got the message and stepped out of the car.

"Jackie, is there any reason anyone would be following you?"

She looked surprised. "No." Jacks had mentioned being careful, and that they should always be in public places.

She didn't see an hour at the shops would be bad, and if Grimaldi or the mob wanted them, they'd have done something before. They must know the police had them, and for all they knew, they were in the cells sleeping. "No, Paul, I don't think anyone would be following me, why?"

Paul nodded. "Okay, no problem. I'll come to the shops with you if that's okay. I fancy a look around."

They headed into the shopping centre. Jackie was in 'attack dog mode'.

"So, Rone, let's get something for you first; shoes, then a jacket, underwear, socks and some winter shoes or boots." They headed into Levi's first; she had him in four pairs of jeans before he begged to be allowed the 501s, and could he have that shirt? Essentially, they kitted him out in almost one store. Next, John Lewis, Boots, M&S. She was a whirlwind. Sofia was in and out of changing rooms. Rone could hardly believe the amount of things Jackie had them try on. Rone found a shop with New York Yankees baseball caps. Could he have a blue one?

Jackie smiled away. "I'm more a Metz fan, but fine."

He bought the world's amount of check shirts; a lamb's wool-lined Levi's jacket was by far his favourite thing, and in Clarks, he found another pair of 'desert wellies'.

Paul approved. "Nice look, son, like that."

Paul was always slightly in the background, followed along and slowly became a bag carrier for Sofia and Jackie. He even cracked the odd smile at Rone being made to try on stuff he'd never wear.

Jackie had smashed the credit card. The 'guys' were set.

"Okay, let's go or Jacks would be having a fit."

They'd meet him back at the house. Paul stashed all the bags in the boot, and the BMW headed out into the late afternoon traffic. He'd not spotted the Capri, and as it got darker, he'd struggle to distinguish the headlights from the other cars.

He made a snap turn to the left without indicating, he was driving a BMW after all…he accelerated down the street, turned left again and again, then back onto the main road. There, about four cars up was a blue Capri. Gotcha!

"He does that," said Jackie, smiling away, "seems to be his thing."

Paul smiled back. And they headed to Jacks home.

In the meantime, Jacks had been busy. He'd explained everything to Harry regarding Grimaldi, and the fact they were looking for him. He was pretty sure he'd gone to ground. Harry had found them a place to stay; they were to go to a place in the country close to Rone's granddad's place, on a farm. Harry had been busy and arranged with a farmer his dad had worked for, an old friend, to rent a small tied cottage which sat at the end of a lane, past the farmhouse. To get to the cottage, you had to pass through two gates and the farmyard with its two dogs.

"Better than any alarm," Harry had thought.

The cottage was at the confluence of a stream and a river; they made a natural barrier. If anyone wanted to get to the house, one way in, one way out. The only people who knew where they would be were Rone, Sofia, Jacks and Harry. Jacks wasn't sure he trusted Carl enough to tell him. He'd fill Jackie in; she was more than trustworthy. Time to implement the plan.

Chapter 14
Hiding in Plain Sight

Jacks was waiting at home when they got back. They piled everything on the sofa. Irene was having a bit of a 'house tidy' moment. The 'guys' would need to get packed. Rone had even picked up a bag, so they got busy chopping off price tags and getting things put away. Irene wanted to wash everything, but no time, they had to get on. Harry was to meet them in a couple of hours off the motorway, and they'd get to the cottage. Paul was sitting at the table having a cup of tea. Irene had insisted; he looked as if he'd possibly had enough of shopping and Jackie, poor lad.

Jacks was eyeing him; he didn't look like a normal driver. A bit too switched on, he thought, then filed that away under 'shit to get looked at.' There was almost a holiday atmosphere, and Rone and Sofia looked really happy for the first time in a long time, he thought.

"So, I need you both to listen; we're taking you both out of London. You'll stay on a farm. You're not, under any circumstances, to go running around in the local towns, villages or the pub; especially the pub, Rone. Got it?" Yes, he'd got it.

They didn't know how long they'd be there, they hoped a few days at most. They needed to catch this piece of work

Grimaldi and find out who he worked for and put a stop to him. He was dangerous, very, did they understand? The giggles and humour stopped. They suddenly looked their age, and Jacks took a beat to realise what they were asking of two 18-year-old kids.

"Okay, let's get going, all packed? Good."

There would be supplies at the cottage; Chrissy had taken care of that. She'd done a shop for a week, and even Rone could open a can of beans. Chrissy, Harry and the farmer would be the only contact.

"There's no phone, the nearest is the farm's, but nobody knows you're there. Think of it as a bit of an holiday; it'll soon be Christmas, so you kids can have your own little place to stay."

They were ready to go. Jackie had a moment of pure emotion and hugged them both. She kissed Rone on the forehead.

"Rone, take care of my girl. And, Rone…"

"Yes, Jackie?"

"Take care of yourself."

Paul was watching it all going on; he knew when to keep quiet. Jacks gave him a sideways glance. "You whisper a word, son, and I'll farkin know, you got it?"

Paul nodded. "Yes, inspector." He understood. Was Jackie ready to go to the hotel? She was.

"Okay, we should go." Paul nodded to Jacks.

"Can I have a word?" Jacks was all ears.

"There was a car following us today, know who that might be?"

Jacks gave him another sideways look. "You're a bit sharp, son, ain't cha?"

Paul straightened. "Just observant, inspector."

"What car, colour, make, reg number?"

"Blue Capri, two up, shirts and ties, ring any bells?"

Jacks nodded. "Hmmm, sharp enough, son. They were mine, and who the fuck might you be?"

Paul pulled his cheeks in a little and pursed his lips. "Well, inspector, I'd say I'm on the right side of things, that's all you need to know."

"Understood." Jacks fucking hated 'spooks' always so fucking smart ass. Who'd put him in place? 'Top boss' calling in a favour, he supposed.

In the meantime, two cars had arrived and Parky and Alisha had snuck into the kitchen. There was a deception plan of sorts in place: Parky and Alisha would double as Sofia and Rone, coats on, hoods up, that kind of thing. It was dark out and there were two Ford Grenada's sitting on the drive. Parky and Alisha would be bundled into one, with their bags, and Rone and Sofia into the other. To anyone watching, they'd have to decide which car had the right target. The cars would then split once on the M1; one would speed ahead, the other would loop off at Junction 9, head back towards St Albans, and try to disappear as best it could.

The other would then take Junction 10, into Dunstable and back around towards the A5; it would then loop back onto the motorway. It wasn't very elegant, but the best they could do for now. Harry was waiting at junction 13, there'd be no stopping, just a light flash, and on to the farm. Jackie and Paul made their way to the BMW.

"Okay, Jackie?"

"Yes, Paul. Can we head back by the way of a pub please, I need a very large drink."

"Yes, Jackie, not a worry." He knew just the place.

The big Fords hit the M1 and speeded up, running in convoy, at the allotted junction. The rear car peeled off, the police radio on the dash clicked twice, Jacks clicked back once on the transmit button. Rone and Sofia were hunkered down in the back of the car; anyone looking in would think there were only two people in the car. They held hands, Rone was having a moment; how the fuck had it gone from a drink on a summer's night, to hiding in a car in a few months? He'd only met her in August, for fuck's sake, mate. This shit needs to calm the fuck down, now they had nutters out to kill them both. The boy who'd been scared of a bag in a tree had come a long way. Yeah, he thought, almost backup the M1 for the first time since the end of September.

Harry was in the lay-by just off the junction. He saw the Ford turn left out of the junction, flash once and he lit the SAAB up. They headed through every back lane he knew, no main drags, as they dropped into the valley. There was a mist forming, and the visibility became a bit limited. Jacks was muttering to the driver about the farkin countryside, how ten miles outside London was nothing but Yokels and village idiots!

They passed through a large country park, wound down through the forest and came to a farm track on the right. The SAAB turned in, splashing through the puddles on the lane. Rone suddenly knew where he was; they were heading for Alex' farm, his dad's mate. Fuck, he had a few memories of tractors, calves and his granddad rushing in, they did a wooshy loop and left him feeling relieved. He gripped Sofia.

"I know where we are."

"Really?"

"Yeah, it's gonna be okay."

He kissed her full on the lips and bounced a little with excitement.

Harry was out undoing the chains on the gates, dogs barking away in the yard to the side, the light clicked on and a hand waved, from an upstairs window. Harry flicked a thumbs up back, and pulling through, he waved the Ford along.

"Up to the yard, mate, I'll see you there."

He beckoned them to follow, and the SAAB weaved down a track to a brick cottage, two up two down. 'Very cosy' is how Jacks would describe it. The lights were on, and Chrissy waited at the door. Everyone piled out of cars. Jacks was shaking Harry by the hand, and Chrissy was bouncing a little on the balls of her feet. She'd not seen Rone in a few weeks, and she'd never met Sofia. She almost leapt on him.

"Easy, Mum, blimey, mate!"

He did his best to hide the emotions but he folded into her arms. Chrissy reached out a hand to Sofia and pulled her in.

"So nice to meet you finally, I'm Chrissy."

Harry was there, he got as emotional as Harry could get.

"You look thin, boy, ain't they feeding you?"

Rone rolled his eyes. Harry had met Sofia, he gave her his best wink, and she smiled back.

"Okay, everyone inside, let's get things sorted."

Chrissy had made a stew; the little kitchen had a wood stove and a fireplace in the living room. The fire was blazing away, the place was warm, but they'd need to keep the fire in. Alex had put plenty of wood in the shed. There was enough milk and they could get that from Alex at the farm; for the rest, Chrissy would call back in the week.

"All set? Come on then, sit down, let's get you fed, and Rone, love, stop mooning around and look after Sofia. She looks proper lost and tired; c'mon, boy chop-chop!"

He rolled his eyes again.

Harry and Jacks were deep in conversation. Yeah, he'd filled Alex in, he knew the score, mate; any strange cars or folks knocking around he knew the number.

About an hour later, they were suddenly alone, they all seemed to depart at the same time. Rone and Sofia were completely alone. Chrissy had washed up for them, and now they sat on the tiny sofa in the tiny living room in front of the fire. His emotions got all wooshy again and spun around to feelings, all sorts of feelings. The girl sitting here with him was the biggest emotional roller coaster he'd ever had to try to understand. Chrissy had put some bottles of Guinness in the fridge; he'd had a couple of those, and Sofia had made sucky faces when she tried it.

"That's awful! Can your mum bring us some wine? I don't think I can survive here without a glass or two of red."

He was smiling at her. She looked up, and as always with Sofia she pulled him into her blue-on-blue eyes.

"What are you thinking?" She asked.

"Is this what life is like? I mean, if we were normal, I'm not sure there's anything normal about us...but I mean, if we were living together, me working on the farm, and walking home down the lane, is this what all that's about?"

"You mean: me home, waiting like a good little woman? Waiting for her hunky farmer?"

Her eyes twinkled, and she grinned.

"No, I mean, what happens next? I'm a bit scared for all that, aren't you?"

She pushed him back into the cushions.

"What happens, Rone, is what we want to happen, can you understand?"

He was pulled into her eyes: she had power over his soul; he was helpless.

"This *will* be over at some point, and I'm coming to terms with that it's changed us forever. By over, I mean the mess that we're surrounded with, not us. No matter what happens, there's always an *us*."

Rone's emotions were making notes at this point; some of this stuff was really good; they were sure they could use it again in the future!

They sat looking into the fire. He threw on another log, and it sent sparks flashing up the chimney. He pulled her in close.

"Remember my first time in your house?"

She smiled.

"We had a bath, and at Jacks' place, we'd had a bath…hmmm…the bath here is really tiny, have you seen it?"

She laughed. "There's no way we can fit in that!"

She was smiling at him, her eyes as bright as he'd ever seen them. Her cheeks flushed a little by the heat from the fire. He pinged a smile out, it bounced right back off hers, and he laughed.

"I'm pretty sure we'd fit, I reckon. It's a tradition now, and we can't break traditions now, can we?" He bounced up, and in his best West country accent, "Come on Mrs Farmer Giles, I reckon you need a good soaking."

She was laughing so hard. "You're an idiot!"

"I knows!" He did strong arm impressions with his puny left arm.

She leapt up, kissed him, held his face. "Take me to my bath, my man! I demand a bath!"

They giggled their way up the stairs to the tiny bath.

Chapter 15
Bits and Bangs

Sapper Bob had a phone round what was left of his old team. He'd asked about sources for RDX; it was still uncertain where the explosive had come from. He, Chris and Terry had the contents of the evidence bag on a table. There wasn't much left: the cone had been added to bits of battery, a small part of what looked like a detonator, some bits of wire very little to go on.

Chris was moving the parts around with the end of a Biro. The detonator cap was fired by a charge from the 6v battery, but the cap was too common a part to make it stand out. Could be from any industrial explosive suppliers, mining companies, and quarries? No, that was nothing to go on. The battery was an Ever Ready 6v radio battery, so again, nothing. The two pieces of wire: Bob was looking at the crimp in the wire where there had been a small connector. The last person to touch that before it went off built the thing. They were also missing any kind of timer or initiator. So another 'how'.

He'd get the boys together, have a curry and see if they could shine any thoughts on things. All of the team were veterans of various conflicts.

"You boys up for a few beers and hear a bunch of old gits talk war stories?"

The lads laughed. "You need help with the Zimmer, mate, or will you cope getting to the pub?"

Parky had been busy, not just supplying his boss with endless cups of tea. He'd been shaking a few trees regarding the bomb. Just getting the word out around various 'bodies', as he liked to call them. Since they'd come to the conclusion that it wasn't terror-related, and probably meant to be used to blow a hole in something, they were looking at banks, but high-value target banks. They would need to have the right amount of money in them to make blowing a hole to get in worthwhile. Or gold, or even diamonds. Had to be high value. This wasn't a post office job brandishing a sawn-off shotgun, so word was out: the 'bodies' were sniffing around.

Bob and the lads had been drinking in the 'The Mother Red Cap' in Camden. They were a few pints in, and tales were getting longer, bangs bigger, and risks taken hairier. Chris and Terry being about half the age of Bob's old crew, sat back and soaked it all up. Along with a few pints, these old fellas could put the ale away! Alf, Cam, Johnny, and Bob had all served in the same unit. Johnny was missing two fingers from his left hand and had been invalided out in the mid-sixties. The rest literally soldiered on, either teaching sprogs like Terry and Chris, or lads and lassies from the Royal Engineers. Bob thought Johnny was a bit off his game: normally when they had a few beers, he'd be pulling the finger story out of the bag, how he'd fucked up handling a blasting cap, the fucker went pop, and popped his fingers off. But he was a bit quiet tonight.

They ended up in the curry house just down from the pub. After a few more beers, Alf and Cam were getting on with the youngsters. They were pulling the bones out of the information regarding the pub bomb. It didn't really do to talk about it in the restaurant, but they seemed to be the only ones in on a Wednesday night, 'tomorrow's a school day' an all that. Alf was nodding away as Terry span the story up.

"You reckon it was shaped?"

"Bob's thoughts; yeah, mate, shape cone, bowl."

They reckoned on at least enough explosives to make a big hole in a strong wall. It had made a proper mess of the inside of the pub, and the folks who were within blast range, but most had been killed by debris, as was nearly always the way.

Cam spoke up, "I reckon someone fucked up, mate."

He had their attention.

"How so, Cam?"

"Well, mate, they initiated it by either being clumsy fuckers, or they didn't keep the battery and initiator separate. I've seen it, we had a bloke in Londonderry do it once. You only tend to do that kind of thing once, he was no exception, but we had enough of the bomb remains to put the story together. Weren't not putting him back together…hahaha, he filled a fucking shoe box when they buried him."

They'd reached the dark humour stage of the evening drinking. Bob was chuckling away. "Shoebox…you fucker, Cam," but his thoughts made sense.

Carl was back in the UK. He'd flown into Heathrow and caught a cab home. He'd arrived at Portland Place to find Mrs Dodds up to her elbows in fingerprint dust. She'd been cleaning for two days.

"They'd made a dreadful mess, Mr Nyman."

She thought he looked unwell and had become more unwell when he saw the covering door to the wall safe was open!

"There's a number here for you to call Mr Nyman an Inspector Jacks."

Carl's head was spinning.

"Ah, Mr Nyman, we've been waiting for you to get in touch. I take it you're back in the UK. Had you left a forwarding number, we'd have contacted you sooner. Yes, do you think you can come down to the station? We need to have a little chat."

Jacks heard the clicking sound and knew they were being listened to. His daughter? Yes, she was safe. No, he couldn't tell him where she was, but she was safe. No, he was sure he couldn't speak to her just now, she was safe. Let's leave it at that, shall we? Could he come right away?

"Fine, I'll expect you within the hour."

Carl had gone to the safe, pressed the code in, taken a deep breath and pulled the door. It was empty. A small note read: 'Please contact DI Jacks!' If that was his sense of humour it was very twisted.

Carl needed to move fast. If they had the safe contents, they must know something, or they've been their usual nosey fucking selves and started adding things up. But how? His thing was financial, nothing to do with bombs or Sofia, and why were they in the house? The proverbial penny had yet to drop. He was flapping way too hard for it to hit the ground.

He took a taxi to the police station, asked for Jacks and was shown through. Jacks was at his chaos-strewn desk, Parky on the other side. He was rolling a cigarette licking the paper and closing up. Carl looked a mess. Any composure he'd had before was still on the carpet with his dignity, he wasn't in a good place.

He was burbling at Jacks, "Is this some kind of joke?"

Parky raised his eyebrows.

Jacks took a sip of tea: "Joke, Mr Nyman? Which part? The part where a known criminal has access to your house, via the keys he took from your daughter when she was unconscious after a bomb attack? The part where he's taken items of her clothing or the part where we find a half million pounds in your safe?"

Carl swallowed hard. "Who is this person who's been in my house?"

That's your question? Jacks thought. "I think we'd better go and have a sit down somewhere a little more private, like a nice comfy interview room. Would you come along, sir, please?"

"Am I under arrest?"

"No, sir, not at all, just need things a little more formal."

Carl was trying to add up the pieces, but his normally ordered brain wasn't putting square things in square holes; it was trying to ram in circles, and nothing worked. Jacks sat on the other side of a small table. Parky leant against the wall puffing on the roll up and trying to keep it alight. No tea request yet. Things were serious.

Jacks was getting the story out as he saw it. Carl sat back trying to stop the relentless hammering of blocks in the wrong holes. Jacks was finishing up, "So at that point, Mr Nyman, we put your daughter and Rone Brennan in protective custody."

Carl snapped back, "You've locked them up? How dare you?"

Jacks had the weakest of smiles. Emotion. That's good; they were pressing the right buttons.

"So given this man has been in your house on more than one occasion, we're wondering why. Why Sofia, and the fact he'd gone in on the prowl after the explosion, and taken the necklace from her, and the watch from Rone, and then he'd taken more of her things from the house. Why would that be, sir? Do you owe this man money, or is there something deeper than that?"

Carl was rattled at this point. "I don't know why anyone would take my daughter's underwear!"

Jacks eyes widened. "I don't recall mentioning her underwear, sir. Would you like to expand on your statement there?"

Carl was visibly shaking. He knew that his level of fucking up was in orbit, it was that high.

Grimaldi was in a bedsit on the Great North Road, dingy shit tip of a place. He wasn't impressed with where they'd put him; the landlady smelled of cat piss, and the wallpaper was peeling in the corner of the room due to the damp. He wouldn't put up with this for long. The phone in the hallway was ringing. He sat up on the bed. He heard the old woman answer, and then she was calling up the stairs, "Mr Michael, the phone. The phone for you, dear?"

He swung off the bed and was down the stairs in a couple of bounds. It was his 'contact': "Go to the phone box at the bottom of the road, ten minutes."

Grimaldi was back pulling his shoes on and heading out the door, head down, collar of his coat pulled up. The phone box barely had windows and smelled like a urinal, which in some ways, it was. He picked up the phone, put his finger on the cradle and waited; the first ring, he answered. "Yes?"

"Nyman is back. He's with the police."

"Yes and?" The question hung briefly and then the gravity of it brought it crashing down.

"He's been there all afternoon, so we imagine he's being cooperative, shall we say? We need you to go and find out how cooperative he's been. Is that understood?"

"But they are looking for me…"

The voice let the moment pass. "We'll take care of you. We need you to understand there's bigger things at stake here than your liberty, do you understand?"

He felt the hairs on the back of his neck stand up. Yes, he understood, he'd get on it. He understood how disposable he was.

They had left Carl Nyman sweating on his own for fifteen minutes. Jacks had called 'top boss' and wanted to set up a proper interview and to get all on tape. He felt sure Nyman would spill.

"Get a couple of brews, Parky, let's get back in."

Carl wanted to know if he was under arrest.

"No, sir, anything you tell us is at your own discretion. We don't have grounds to arrest you on any charge. We'd like some parts of the story filled in, the money for example, and the connection to Grimaldi."

Carl had paled a little at the mention of the name. They didn't know if he knew of him, or if there was something else.

Carl looked more composed when they returned. Parky thought they'd fucked up by giving him a bit of space to calm down. Jacks thought he just looked a bit smug.

"Why did you open the safe, inspector? Would that not count as an illegal search of my property?" Jacks had been waiting for this one. "We weren't searching your house, Mr

Nyman. We were searching for evidence of a dangerous intruder, and our forensics team noticed the covering door ajar. They merely opened the doors."

Jacks was lying his tits off, but it stalled Carl momentarily. He was looping his mind back to the last time he'd been to the safe, and who's to say that Sofia or the 'boy' had not opened the covering door? But he was sure he'd closed everything. You don't bugger off on business and leave a half million pounds free to walk out the door with a couple of kids.

He was flat. He hadn't anything more to say. He wanted to know where she was and why they wouldn't tell him.

"Again, Carl, she's safe and we appreciate your concern, but we feel the fewer people who know the better and safer things are for Rone and Sofia."

"So they're together?"

Jacks gave himself an internal punch in the face; fuck, shit. "I can't say, Carl, they're safe."

Carl took three hours to give up Farina, the London side of the operation and his level of involvement. The pressure of it all was too much. Farina had scared him. He'd made him sick with his threats to harm Sofia, and his lewd comments about her. Carl was a dick, but he was also a father. He didn't feel much like knowing Sofia would come to real harm because of him. He wasn't prepared for the level of violence that was happening around his family, and he didn't believe Farina when he said the bomb wasn't their doing. They were capable of anything, and thirty-two lives taken was nothing for these people. They cared about nothing and nobody, money and power, and he'd been pulled down to their depths and wasn't able to see the surface.

Jacks knew they had to move and move fast. He needed to brief everyone. 'Top boss' was making calls to various departments, and they had spooled up the machinery to go forward. They needed to sting those involved, but they needed to move with caution. It couldn't be obvious that Carl had given them up. Jacks had thought the risk of letting him go home too great; but if they kept him, then it was obvious and those involved would vanish. They had to let him go home; they'd have to put a team in place, but covert. He was pulling it all together.

The team for the house was in the back of a van. They'd parked just at the end of the road, so they could watch the front door, and Nyman had been told to move around as normal. They had him covered; four lads from the firearms team sat in a car on the road that led to Portland Place. Both the teams had been briefed on Grimaldi; they had a small photo of him pinned to the dash. He was the main threat; he knew the house, knew Nyman. If anyone was coming for him, it would be Grimaldi.

Parky had driven Nyman home. He'd been silent all the way. Parky gave him the brief, "Act as normal as possible, tomorrow go to the office, call as many people as he can tonight and keep their wiretap busy. If you're on the phone a lot, they will have resources tied up, and they'd be waiting for information before they moved."

Did he understand? He did. His thought process now was one of getting through the next few hours and not fucking up, but a bit of his dignity had crawled up from the floor, and it felt a bit more comfortable than before.

He dropped him at the door. Okay, they would be in touch. He was as safe as he could be. There were teams looking out for him. Carl was not so sure he felt at all safe.

Grimaldi had made his way down to the back of the house. Jacks team had fucked up. They'd not secured the area at the back of the house. They'd thought access that way was not really possible, you had to go through too many places, but Grimaldi had spent time working out a route. He'd planned to get to Sofia when the time was right; now he was putting that planning to use to get to Nyman himself.

He dropped into the small garden and felt his way forward. There was enough light from the light in the kitchen to see Nyman preparing a drink, taking ice from the fridge and pouring Scotch into a glass.

"Patience now, wait for the time, let him relax."

Grimaldi had on a black ski mask and black leather gloves and he had a razor-sharp switchblade ready. He needed to stay calm. He was controlling the moment, taking his breathing down and keeping his heart rate under control. Nyman was back in the lounge. Grimaldi had the kitchen door open in just a few seconds, and he was cat-like in his movements. Nyman sat with his back to the kitchen door, the TV on. He'd forgotten to get on the phone; he just wanted a stiff drink.

The knife clicked open, and less than a second later, Grimaldi was behind Carl, his hand over his mouth and the blade hovering just in front of his right eye.

"Shhhhhhhshhhh, now, let's not make the mistake of moving, eh? I'm gonna stay here, the knife is staying in front of your fuckin eyeball, you make a sound and I'll stab you through it into your brain, do you understand?"

Carl took a small breath through his nose and tried to nod, his mind trying to comprehend the level of madness that was going on at this time.

"Now, I'm going to move my hand. If you make a sound, you're dead before you hit the floor. If you move funny, you're dead before you hit the floor. Are we fucking clear, Nyman?"

He was crystal.

"I'm going to ask a series of questions, you're going to answer. Is that clear as well?"

Very.

"You were with the police all afternoon; what did they talk about? The weather, the football, or about a certain group that owned his fucking arse?"

"We talked about my daughter."

"Ahhh, the lovely Sofia. And where is she, Carl? Is she upstairs, can I go pay her a visit? I do have plans for Sofia; we're going to have fun together, me and her."

"Fuck you," Carl spat the words out, "fuck you, I'll fucking kill you!"

"Big words for a man with a knife at his face, Carl. Now, tell me about our friend Jacks and his merry bunch of fuckers."

Carl had his brain racing. The blocks were back and he needed them to fit; he had to calm down to make something sound convincing for this madman.

"We talked about the bombing, about the events surrounding the bomb," and his daughter was missing. He span out lie after lie. Grimaldi said nothing. He let him flail on with a story that at this point Carl didn't believe either. He was trying for time, hoping that the police would knock, or someone would call to check on him. None of those things happened. He felt the time draining away.

"I'm going to cut you Carl," Grimaldi hissed out the words, "I'm going to cut you just enough to be painful, just so you realise you're fucking pissing me off, do you understand?"

Carl was taking short breaths, his brain collapsing. Grimaldi flicked the blade and cut him down the side of his face, his hand back covering his mouth as he did so. Carl wriggled and tried to cry out, but the hand clamped harder.

"Now, Carl, let's have it again, the story where you told them nothing."

He cut him again, the blood running down over the gloves, making Carl's face slippery.

This went on for twenty minutes. Eventually, Carl gave in; the pain was too much. He told Grimaldi everything. He'd reached the point where he knew no matter what he did, he was going to die. He accepted the fate. He tried to sit up on the sofa and have a straight back for what was coming, but Grimaldi had one more twist.

"Where was dear Sofia?" He hissed.

Carl didn't know, and this time he really didn't know. A flick of the blade, more pain.

"Is she with the boy?"

Flick.

"Were they with the police?"

Flick.

Carl was holding onto consciousness, just.

Grimaldi flicked again.

"She's with the boy, isn't she? I'm gonna make him watch, Carl when I have my time with her. I'm gonna make him watch."

The front of Carl's shirt was soaked in blood, it drained through onto the sofa.

"Fuck you, just fuck you!"

Grimaldi smiled under the mask. "Hmmm, Carl…I don't think you'll be fucking anybody, but I might." With that, he cut down the inside of his left arm. He cut the Brachial artery with the skill of a surgeon. "All over, Carl."

He wiped the blade on the sofa and was out the back door. Carl was dead before he'd left the building.

Chapter 16
Farm Life

Rone was at the bedroom door. The December weather brought a cold wind from the east; the windows in the cottage were pre-war, and that meant the first one, not the second! It was chilly inside.

He'd watched her sleep for a while, and then got out of bed, pulling on a sweatshirt. He'd gone down to clean and light the fire; he'd found kindling in the barn, got the kitchen stove going and then lit the fire in the living room. After the house in London, this place felt prehistoric.

He'd got the kettle going and made coffee. His mum had bought non-sliced bread; I mean, what was she thinking? He cut 'door stops' and made toast and piled on some butter and marmalade. He balanced it all precariously on a big plate and weaved his way up the narrow stairs.

He took a moment at the doorway, just to watch her for a few seconds. He thought she was incredibly beautiful. The feelings swooped and dived around inside his mind; they gave him a warm glow, which made him smile. He really liked that feeling. The feelings settled down on a branch and waited.

He dropped into his 'farmer Giles' West Country accent, "Ere, missus, I's bought you'se some corffee." She was awake, laughing.

"What a way to wake up! C'mon, village idiot, come and get back in bed."

He handed across the mug of coffee, and she took a sip, "Hmmm, nice. Oh and deformed toast! You're so special, thank you!"

He grinned and climbed back into the small double bed. It had an eiderdown and an old mattress and the frame and springs creaked when they moved. It was hilarious and made them laugh all the more.

"It's cold out, the wind blows hard here in the winter. But we could go for a walk in the forest. Nobody said we couldn't go for a walk. I can check with Alex, but the forest is huge; goes on for miles."

She was sipping her coffee and munching the 'door-stop toast.' "Mmmm, lovely, so much bread, Farmer Giles. You did so well! I'm not sure I'll be able to move, but a walk sounds amazing."

Washed, dressed and wrapped up, they walked up the track to the farm. The main house sat off to the left as you came up from the cottage; not a big place, a typical estate farmhouse, big enough for the tenant farmer and a family. Alex lived alone there now, his wife having passed away some years before. On the right side stood the milking parlour. Alex still kept a herd of around sixty Friesian cows. The winter was here, and they were inside the large barn on the track up to the main yard.

Alex was in the yard with a small red tractor stacking bales on the buck rake at the back: flat cap, green overalls, and wellies covered in cow shit. Yep, he was just as Rone remembered him. Two border collies ran around but stayed close to his feet.

He looked up. "Morning, young Rone, morning, Miss."

Sofia reached out her hand. "I'm Sofia." He did a slight nod as he shook her hand. "Very Victorian," she thought. His hands were calloused and hard. Were all country folk this way? She'd been to Anne Marie's place plenty of times; they all seemed to drive BMWs and roar around in Land Rovers and big green tractors.

"How are the cows, Alex?" Rone smiled up.

Alex had a quizzical look on his face. "How are they, young Rone? Black and white and in the barn is how they are. You're full of daft questions, youngun!"

Sofia was in stitches laughing, Rone blushing away.

Alex laughed. "I'm only messin'. Head on up to the big barn; they've all changed since last you were here. Hector is still there though, boy, watch him, he's in the pen on his own at the back. You remember the rules around Hector, boy?"

Rone did; never get arms inside the pen, rub his forehead, scratch between the eyes. Don't ever get body parts between him and the rails.

Sofia was looking at him with questioning eyes. "Who in the world is Hector?"

Aha, Rone would show her. "Let's go and say hello to the ladies."

"Ladies? This place is full of surprises!"

Rone smiled: it was, she'd see. The 'ladies' turned out to be the milking cows. Rone was clicking and clucking to them. The 'ladies' munching on their hay didn't pay him much notice. He reached through and patted some of them, scratching away at their heads. He held some hay, and some took the mouthfuls, munching away. Sofia was seeing a whole different side to him.

He turned. "Go on, give it a try."

She was a bit nervous. "They're so big, I never imagined."

"Go on," he said, "try."

She took up a handful of hay and fed the big bovines through the grill, her eyes wide with the thrill.

"Where's Hector?" She asked.

"Oh I think he's out back in his own pen. He only gets to play with the 'girls' when the time is right."

She laughed. "Does he have a bath he can use?"

Rone was cracking up. "It would be some bath!"

They rounded the corner, and there in his pen was Hector, a full-grown Friesian bull. He was huge, almost a ton in weight.

"My god, he looks like a house!"

"Ah, he's big eh," said Rone. "Come this way. Stay in his line of sight."

He took her hand and led her around to the front of the pen. "My granddad reckons he's a big softy, but they will turn on you. Don't take it for granted that he looks a bit dopy. He's had Alex on the floor almost killed him."

"Really?" Sofia asked.

"Ah, yes, but he's of his way, nothing personal like. Granddad reckoned he'd have had him on some Sunday dinner tables for doing that."

The big bull eyed them and came forward in the pen.

Rone was clicking away at him. "Hey, Hector, hey, Hector." The big bull gave a snort, then put his head forward over the bar of the pen, and Rone gave him a good scratch between the eyes.

Sofia was mesmerised. "I've never been this close to anything as big as him." She reached out and gave him a gentle pat. Hector blew snot out of his nose, and she jumped back! "Oh wow, he's amazing!" Her eyes were wide and the smile beamed out of her face.

"C'mon, let's tell Alex where we're going. If I remember, there's a pond with ducks up in the forest. They put them there for the shooting in the season."

She was lost and her head spinning a little: one-ton bulls, ponds, ducks and shooting. Who was this version of Rone? He seemed to know everything about the farm and the animals. She loved how his face lit up when he patted Hector and 'the ladies'.

"Alex, we wanted to head up to the duck pond, is that okay?"

"Not too far now, Rone. I'll expect you back in an hour, two at the most. If you don't mind and if your arm is up to it, I'd like some help to move some bags of feed that will arrive today. You remember the way though?"

Rone pointed to a spot amongst the trees. "Over the bridge, straight up the track, when you get to the old tin shed, it's the path to the left."

"Okay, lad. Did you put enough wood on the fire?"

Rone looked back at the cottage, smoke drifted up from the chimney. "Dunno, Alex, not sure it will last."

"Well, nip back on the tractor, stoke it up, lad, and then on your way."

His eyes lit up; he hadn't driven anything for so long, and the little Massey Fergusson was one of the first things he had ever driven. "C'mon," he said.

She took a second. "Where do I sit? There's only one seat…"

"On the mudguard, silly!" He said it as if everyone in the world would know to sit on the mudguard!

The little tractor burbled into life at the turn of the key, and they were away back to the cottage. It bumped and swayed its way back along the track, and she was holding onto his shoulder. He looked across; a huge grin on his face. He pulled around in front of the cottage, ran in, threw logs on the fire and kitchen stove and she waited sitting in the driving seat holding the wheel.

"Can you even drive?" He asked.

"No, no time to learn."

"Well then, about time you did."

"Okay."

He explained the clutch, the hand throttle, and the two-gear levers. "You only need second gear and we're in high range." He could have been speaking Dutch. "So, okay, push down the clutch…yep, all the way down." She was almost standing on the pedal. "Now, move the gear lever across and back until you feel it stop. That's it, keep the clutch in. Okay, some throttle." She pulled the lever around a little. "Okay, that's fine. Now, very slowly, let the pedal come up, that's it, bit more, bit more…" The little tractor gave a jump and they were off. She hung onto the steering wheel for all the world. Rone was smiling at her. "Amazing, you're amazing!" He kissed her, and she squealed with excitement.

With a bit of help with the steering, she navigated their way back through the gate and into the yard and he had her push the clutch down. The tractor came to a stop, and he popped it out of gear and they hopped off. She couldn't stop smiling and laughing. "I can drive, I can drive a tractor!"

"Close the gate, Rone put the chain on, there's a good lad." He pulled the gate to, slipped the chain around the post, and popped the bolt through.

Alex watched as they walked over the bridge and up the track towards the forest, hand in hand, chatting, Rone pointing at who knows what. She was looking back at him and it had been a long time, but Alex thought it the nicest thing he'd seen in a while. He went back to work, the collies Jess and Sue always at or around his feet.

In London, the night had not gone well for Jacks team. Their suspicion had been aroused when they saw all the lights had stayed on. At around midnight, one of the car team had done a walk-by: no movement inside.

He was on the radio. "We need to move in, something not right about that."

They were banging on the door, no answer.

"Get on the radio, bring up the other team and for fuck's sake, get hold of Jacks and Parkinson!"

Two of the lads barged the door, and they were in. The TV was on, the sound up—a little loud they thought—and no response from Nyman. Jenks had his weapon drawn, and he sighted once around the door: there was a body on the sofa, the face a mask of blood.

"Fuck!" They rushed in. Carl Nyman sat in a pool of his own blood, his head drooped on his chest and his arm sliced from the armpit to the elbow. Jenks waved back at the others.

"Get the boss! Fuck off and get the boss, and stay out of this fucking room! He's fucked, mate, we need to keep everyone out!" The boys were looking at each other. "We've royally fucked up."

At home, Jacks phone was ringing off the hook. He was fighting off the sleep and fumbling by the bed for the light.

He reached out for the phone, "Yes."

"Guv, it's Parky. You need to get to Nyman's place ASAP. He's dead, Guv. I'm on my way there now. Yes, the boys are inside. No, they didn't touch anything. Yes, they're sure he's dead, no doubt. What? No, they reckon a couple of hours at least. Guv, I need to get going. I'll see you there."

Jacks dropped the phone, picked it back up and called 'top boss.' "Sorry, boss, Nyman is dead."

No, he didn't know. Yes, the boys found him. "No, no, no, I don't know how. Parkinson just called me. Yes, I'm on my way."

He was dressed and down the stairs, his head hammering away. "This is a mess, a fucking mess. How could they let him get killed when they sat less than a hundred yards away? What the fuck were they doing?" The rest of his brain was trying to find his car keys and get out the door. Irene stood at the top of the stairs, not the first time she'd been woken up like this.

She'd overheard: "Is it Sofia's dad?"

Jacks flashed her a look, and she took a step back.

"That poor child, what will they do?"

Parky had made the next call to Alisha, "Can you get to Nyman's house?"

"Why?"

"He's dead, mate."

"Shit." Alisha would see him there. "No, keep the scene sterile, no fucking size tens walking through it!" She called two of her team, "Get to the station, pick up the van, full kit, meet me at Nyman's house, and be as quick as you can."

By the time Jacks arrived, the road was sealed off at both ends, blue lights bouncing off buildings, the road full of police vehicles, and an ambulance stood to one side, its blue beacons rotating, and neighbours were out. What on earth was happening? Officers were urging people back inside.

Alisha was on the scene. Parky sat on the kerb; roll up dangling from his fingers, the blue lights flickering in his eyes. He'd seen the body.

Jacks was in front of him. "Parky."

"Guv, it ain't fucking pretty."

He and Alisha did a quick look. The doctor had been in.

"They reckon he's been dead two or three hours at least. The doc's initial thoughts were he'd been tortured for some time, then he'd been cut on the inside of his arm. Doctor reckons whoever did it knew exactly what they were aiming for. Fuck me, Guv, not seen anything quite like that."

Alisha stopped him at the door: "You'll need an overall on."

At the scene of the crime, the guys were getting pictures, the flashes popping off inside the room.

"You reckon it was Grimaldi, Guv?" He knew it was, but how the fuck did he get in, and how the fuck had they missed another way into the house? The back door was slightly open. There was too much to process in one lump, and Jacks needed the chaos in his head to quieten down, just so he could make the decisions in the right order.

Grimaldi had made the call. "It's done." The voice on the end of the phone wanted to know details of what Nyman had said to the police.

"Everything. He'd told them everything, names, dates, places. The police had been to the offices yesterday and taken files and papers. The old Bill knows where you are. You should get on the move. Plenty of time for that, we know what to do."

Did he find the girl?

"No, they've put them in hiding, but outside London." He didn't know where, if they had sources inside the Met, they'd better start using them to find her. Grimaldi already had a suspicion they were near where the boy came from.

They reached the tin hut, and Rone was chatting away about pheasants and different birds. The wildlife and the trees.

She was smiling away. "It's like a day out with Richard Attenborough," she said. "Where does all this come from, Rone?"

"Oh, you know, time on the farm with granddad. I was always here when I was little."

The path led off to the left after the hut, and they pushed on. The climb was a little steeper, and a bit slippery. He'd made a walking stick from a piece of branch, and the path was narrow, so they walked in single file.

He held the stick back behind him. "Grab on, I'll pull you along, it's not too far now."

The wind whistled through the trees and their noses and cheeks were red from the cold and the climb. As they crested the hill, there, on the edge of the trees was a pond, and as promised, there were about twenty or thirty ducks.

Rone dropped into a crouch and pulled her down. "Nice and quiet." They hunkered down in the long grass and watched the ducks doing duck-type things.

"I always thought it must be odd being a duck, your ass in the water all day!"

She was laughing again. Looking into his face, the green flecks in his eyes stood out in the light. She turned back to the pond, let out a breath, and felt completely happy and content. "I'm getting chilly, can we head back?"

He stood up, and the duck alarm system was up and alert. He clapped his hands and almost as one, the ducks scrambled across the water to take off.

There was a big team assembled at the police station. 'Top boss' and David Mc Nee were there. Jacks was briefing everyone in the room. Parky was handing out papers and arrest warrants. They had to act fast. It was 5:30 in the morning; they were each assigned a target address.

"Now, some of these are just suits who work in the company." He didn't think they'd be any threat when the knocks came, some they'd take when they arrived at the office. The bigger concern was some of the mob; they would present different challenges. Airports, ferries and any other way out of the country were on high alert; they'd struggle to get out, even with the head start they had on the police.

Mc Nee was standing, he addressed the room, "Everyone, this is the biggest challenge we've faced in some time, please be alert. We don't need anything else going wrong here. We need the people responsible for this hideous act. That leads me to this character: Grimaldi. I don't want any heroics with him, do not tackle this man if you are alone or separated from your colleagues. Is that clear? This man is our top priority, he's clearly highly dangerous. DI Jacks feels his next act will be to go after Jackie Nyman, or their daughter Sofia. We need to find him. Let's get some doors knocked and find this bastard." Mumbles and nods of approval. The room emptied as if it was on fire.

It had taken Jacks some hours to pull everything together. Parky, his stalwart, was running the phones, relentlessly chasing different departments. The station was buzzing with officers from all over London. Grimaldi was their main concern.

He called Harry. He normally left very early with the lorry; he hoped to catch him before. At number 67, the phone rang as Harry was about to head out. He jumped at the sound, his hand hovering over the receiver. Thoughts scrambled around inside his head; they were jumping to all sorts of conclusions, some of them could jump higher than others, and Harry pounced on the phone. "Yes."

"Harry, Jacks. Carl Nyman was murdered last night."

Harry did a couple of breaths in. How, where, etc. raced around his brain and couldn't find a way out.

"If it's this piece of shit Grimaldi, you could be the next target. He'll try to find Sofia and Rone. No, mate, he's beyond a wrong'un. He's unhinged, mate and he's got some kind of twist on for that girl. No, I don't know. I just think he's a fucking psycho. We need to get you and Chrissy away somewhere. The information for your address and so on is easy to find. Give me some time, Harry, I'll call you back."

Harry grunted a response. He was calling up to Chrissy: "Love, we need to pack a bag. Can you wake Nick up?" He'd sleep through bloody war, that boy. He'd have to go with Chrissy.

Jacks next call was to get someone to Jackie's hotel. They needed her informed of the murder, but they needed to get her some protection. They didn't know if she was in danger, but couldn't take any chances. He sent two of his young detective constables. "She is a firebrand, so expect her to make a fuss. No, they weren't close, but you never know how these things pan out. Be straight and to the point. Okay, all good, now fuck off. Call me when it's done. Let me know what she says."

Harry had some steps out and the loft hatch open.

Chrissy was busy putting things in a case. "Where we going, Harry? What about Rone and Sofia? Don't we need to go there and look after them?"

Harry was mumbling back through the loft hatch. He was in an old army duffle bag, pulling out some odd bits of uniform. His hand found what he was looking for a box. Inside, a well-oiled cloth. Inside that, an American Air Force issued sidearm and two clips. Bullets for the gun were in the bottom of the box, 7 to a clip, 8 bullets if he chambered a round. He fed the bullets into both clips, dropped the other bullets into his pocket and checked the action on the pistol. He'd no time to clean it, but the oiled cloth had kept it in working order, no rust. "Let the fucker come," he muttered, "I'll show that fucker 'unhinged'."

Chapter 17
Boss?

Parky was feeling the strain. By about 8:30, teams had hit doors and the first arrests were made. The work was only going to ramp up from here. He felt a bit fucked, hadn't slept and the image of Carl Nyman was on loop feed at the front of his mind. He was sick of coffee. "Bollocks, I'll get a bite to eat and have a sit down for five minutes." His thinking process felt like it was wading through mud.

He leant forward, pulled open the draw and reached for the tobacco tin. The roll-up process was just beginning and the phone rang. He was at the point where you needed both hands and as he tried to finish the roll up and get the phone he dropped everything. "Bollocks! Yes, Parkinson. What? Who? Dunno put him through." The voice on the other end of the phone was muffled and sounded odd. Parky was too tired to think. "Yes, DC Parkinson, what can I do for you?"

"You're the one on the bomb, ain't ya?"

Parky sat up. "Maybe. What's on your mind?"

"Well son, little bird tells me you're after the blokes what had the fing made. I happens to know one of the blokes got killed when that fing went orf in the pub, mate. So, you find him, an' you'll likely find the rest what did it."

The phone went dead. Parky suddenly wasn't tired. After two months, it was the first break.

He was chasing down the corridor. Jacks was in a side room with 'top boss'.

Parky tapped, didn't wait and barged in, "Guv, I just got a lead on the bombing!"

"Really, what lead? It couldn't have come yesterday, could it? Fuck me, like we don't have enough on. Go on then, son; tell us what you've got."

Parky told of the call. "So what I can make of that is that one of the bods who had the bomb made was killed in the explosion. So we need to go through all the names of the dead, see who has a file or is known to us and then put the associates of that person together. It's the first thing we've had, Guv, eh? Could be something, could be nothing, but it's better than the dose of fuck all that we've been dealing with."

Harry, Chrissy and Nick were in the lorry: where better to be? Anyone looking for them would need to find a Volvo lorry amongst thousands of others on the road, so try and find him. And it would take a genius to work out where Rone and Sofia were. Seems it didn't take a genius, just a bent copper on their payroll.

They were headed up to Birmingham with a load of bricks. They would deliver those, and Harry would drop Chrissy and Nick at her sister's.

"No, you'll be safe there, ain't no way that anyone could find you."

As they headed up the motorway, Nick was already asleep on the bunk!

Harry would head back and leave the trailer in a spot near the farm, and he'd call to check in with Alex. He could sleep in the cab if he had to; if he backed it into the barn nobody would know he was there. He can keep an eye out for anyone coming to the farm. No, he was going to be fine. This nutter had to get caught at some point, half the 'old bill' in the country was chasing him; the other half knew who he was.

Grimaldi was to check in with his contact at 11:00 am. He'd burnt the clothes from the murder, washed the knife in the canal, and rinsed the blood off his hands.

In the boot of the Vauxhall, he had a clothes bag and a stash of clothing. He'd changed into jeans and a blue roll-neck and pulled a peaked cap on. He was in a phone box outside a cafe on the A40, picked the phone up with a piece of cloth and dialled the number. "It's me."

The voice on the other end didn't sound as calm as normal. He guessed they didn't have as much under control as they thought.

"Where's my money?"

"Your money is with the Landlord at the North London Tavern on Kilburn High Road. Get out of London."

"Nyman's daughter, any word on that?"

"She's on a farm."

"Where?"

The voice gave the location. "They're in a small place, secluded, and shouldn't be too difficult. Once that's done, our business is concluded. Do you understand?"

He put on a pair of glasses; they had no lenses but changed the profile of his face, turned the car around and headed for Kilburn.

Rone and Sofia were back at the farm. They'd helped Alex with the bags of feed, tidied up around the yard, and Rone was sweeping out the feed store. Clouds of old straw dust hung in the air, and Sofia was waving her hands around as it got up her nose and in her eyes. "Hang on, Farmer Giles," she mocked, "I don't reckons I can hardly breathe!"

He was laughing away, and then chasing her around the store with the brush.

Alex was at the door. "C'mon, you two, we'll have a bite to eat and a cup of tea. Come to the house when you're ready."

He finished sweeping the floor, leant the brush in the corner and caught her hand in his. "Come along now, Mrs Farmer Giles, give I a kiss!"

The eyes were back doing full deep dive sweeps, and she pulled him close and kissed him.

She brushed straw from his hair. "You look like Wurzel Gummidge!" She swept the dust off his shoulder, placed her hand on his face and breathed out very slowly. "I love you, Rone." His eyes closed for a second. She'd said it before when she was half asleep, but here she was looking into his eyes.

He could see the love. "I love you too."

"Would you really marry me for Marmite?" She asked.

He kissed her again, "In a heartbeat!"

With the case against the mob unfolding and having made a series of arrests that morning, the various teams were each involved in the task of questioning suspects and pulling evidence together. It was quite a haul of influential members of one of London's biggest crime syndicates. They had a long way to go, but Nyman had been exact with his information and had placed incriminating documents in safe places; it was all falling into place. Alisha and the team were still at the house, Grimaldi had left bloody footprints on the floor and glove marks on the door on the way out; no prints of course. But they'd been able to piece together his route by the blood on walls and fences. What they needed was a car; had anyone seen anything? Appeals were going out on the TV news; there was an out-of-date photo of Grimaldi. If the public sees this man, they are asked to call the number at the bottom of the screen. Under no circumstances are they to approach him or try to apprehend him.

The two officers had called on Jackie at the hotel. She was waiting in the lobby for her driver.

They took her to one side. "Mrs Nyman, we have to inform you that Carl Nyman was murdered last night." She barely moved.

"Mrs Nyman?"

"Yes, I heard you, thank you. Very well, I must get on. I have meetings today and I must head back to New York tomorrow."

The officers looked at each other. They were more shocked by her lack of emotion than anything else. "You realise he's been killed, Mrs Nyman?"

"Yes, I got it. What did you want me to do?"

"Ummm…DI Jacks thought you may be in danger Mrs…" she snapped off the rest of the name.

"Stop calling me that, I'm in no danger. Why would I be? I've nothing to do with him, his business or his dealings, so let me get on with my day. Tell Jacks I'll call him. I need to get to my daughter and get her away from all this. Now go away, let me get on."

Paul was outside with the BMW. He'd witnessed the two officers in conversation with Jackie; he did the sucking in of the cheeks, the pursing of the lips. *Their plan is unravelling*, he thought.

Harry was on his way back down the M1. He had the big Volvo pushing on, he'd be at the farm before it was dark. He had to get back in touch with Jacks and see if they'd caught this bastard yet. He'd stop at Watford Gap Services to see if he could get him on the phone. Someone somewhere had to know something. Jacks wasn't available.

"Could he call back?"

"Is Parkinson there?"

"No, he's tied up, I'm afraid."

"Shit, okay." He'd try later. He had to get to the farm. He headed back out onto the motorway. Spinning the Volvo up, he had her rolling again; the empty flatbed trailer occasionally bounced, and brick dust came up from between the boards. 45 minutes, an hour he'd be there.

Grimaldi had no idea where the place was, he needed directions. All he had was a farm name, and it was in the middle of nowhere. He kept the speed so that he rolled along and made time with the traffic, nothing to make him stand out. Could he risk stopping and buying a map? He'd have to. He eyed the bag of money on the seat. He'd earned all that the hard way, and even though he'd been paid, the next part was all for his own enjoyment. She was going to be a luxury item. He was almost salivating with expectation.

They'd had lunch with Alex, and wandered back down the track to the cottage, hand in hand, chatting about everything and nothing at all.

"Do you think you'll go back to live with your dad?" He asked.

She wasn't sure. "We need to get past this, Rone, get to a point where everything stops being a bit insane." Maybe they could get away and take some time to reflect. She had to understand if she wanted to perform again, and if she could. She loved the theatre and loved performing, but at the moment it was emotionally beyond her.

"And you?"

"I don't have a clue. I need a direction; I need to know where my life goes with you. This is the first time we've thought beyond this, almost like we didn't dare." His doubts about the future were in the flower patch having a good stamp around; they didn't seem to like the colours and happiness.

The fires were salvageable and Rone topped them up, flames sputtering and sparking. "I don't want to think too much beyond today, or tomorrow. I don't need that worry in my head." He looked sad and vulnerable. They sat on the little sofa. Rone had his thoughts in the flames.

She stroked the side of his face, all the seriousness welled up and he bit his lip. "Sorry, that was all a bit much," and his emotions showed up and pumped out a few tears. They dropped on the mat, and she leant in, pulled him close, and wiped them away with her fingers: "Don't cry, I'm not going anywhere without you by my side. It doesn't matter what we do, doesn't mean we can't be together. There's always a way for us." He leant back into her, and they held onto each other as tight as they could.

Grimaldi was looking at the address: Park Farm. Did it mean it's near a park? He saw a sign for the postal town on the address. It was off the motorway at Junction 13, and a signpost for a safari park. Park Farm: bit obvious really. He'd head that way, he had to be able to get directions. The light was fading and the afternoon rolled into early evening. He needed it to be dark. He could approach the place, scope out where they were; get the 'lay of the land' so to speak. As he passed along the road heading for the park, there was a small garage on the left. He'd ask, worth the risk. He pulled in and there was a small kiosk to pay for fuel; an old fella was working under an old Morris van in the workshop attached, and Grimaldi stood in the doorway so he was framed against the light and a silhouette.

"Can I help, mate?"

"Yes, I'm looking for Park Farm; seem to be a little lost."

"Ah, you're not so far." He gave the directions, and Grimaldi thanked him for his time. Not so hard; now to get parked up, and wait for the darkness.

He found the farm; it was off the road and down a short track. He couldn't park there; he'd go along a little way and find a place out of the way. Passing the entrance to the farm, he drove for about a quarter of a mile; there was a gateway which was set back from the road; there were trees over the gateway. The leaves had long gone, but once parked up against the wooden gate the car could hardly be seen. He was in the boot again, looking for darker clothing; he didn't need a mask as there would be no witnesses to what he was going to do. He changed and sat back in the car; he'd walk up the side of the road. If any traffic came, he could just brazen it out, some local out walking to the pub.

Harry had left the trailer and was heading down the track to the farm. They had plenty of deliveries with big lorries, and there was no problem getting down to the gateway. Alex was just finished with the milking and the last of the 'ladies' was making her way back to the big barn. He heard the Volvo pull up and was out of the milking parlour wiping his hands.

"What's up? Harry called in for a spot of tea. I'll be with you in a moment, let me hose down and clean up." He saw the look on Harry's face: "Tell me, lad, what's happening?"

"There's some nutter on the loose. He killed Sofia's dad last night, and now he's looking for her and Rone."

"But surely he'd never find them here. I have days when I don't know where I live," he smiled. Harry wasn't smiling back. "I need to get the wagon out of sight. Is there room in the barn?"

"Should be; you can squeeze it in if I move the big tractor out."

"Good, okay. Dunno, Alex, something not right here, got a feeling in the pit of my stomach."

Jacks was waiting for the report of the victims. Parky had detected some help and had them cross-checking files against names. They had two so far, and neither of them fitted the bill; the trouble was, they needed a quicker way to reference the fingerprints of the victims. They had to slog through file after file to pick out known names with records. It could take days.

Harry and Alex moved the tractor out and he backed the Volvo back into the barn. It wasn't possible to see it from the yard; nobody would know it was there. Harry grabbed his bag and headed into the house.

"You going to tell the boy you're here, Harry?"

"No, not for now. Do you still have your shotgun, Alex?"

"Of course, it's under the stairs."

"Got any shot heavier than the stuff you use for rabbits?"

"I've got some 'buckshot' somewhere. C'mon, Harry, it ain't gonna get to shoot nobody is it?" Harry eyed his friend sideways. "Just want to be prepared."

Alex pulled out the shotgun, a normal 12-bore side-by-side double trigger and a box of buckshot. "Can I borrow your old Barbour jacket and I need a hat."

As Alex was searching for a hat, Harry slipped the pistol in the coat pocket with an extra clip. "Where you going?"

"I'm going down, around the side of the field, and hard up against the cottage. There's some cover, I can make a point to watch there. Alex, lock the doors when I'm gone, and make sure the dogs are in the house."

"You're making me worried, Harry."

"I know, old mate, but I have a feeling about that fucker. Where's the phone?"

He tried Jacks again and finally got through.

He sounded exhausted. "Harry, what's happening?"

"I'm at the farm, have you caught him yet?"

"No, he's still at large. We have London locked down, Harry."

"Jacks, get some local plod here. I'm going to keep an eye on the kids. I don't like any of this. Chrissy? No, mate she's in Coventry with her sister, she's out of the way."

Jacks called his contact in Bedfordshire police and filled him in on what he could. Okay, they'd send a car to nose around. Did he really think he could find them?

"Dunno, he found his way into a fucking house that almost had no way into from the back, so anything was possible. He's a dangerous fucker, so your boys need to take care."

Harry pulled on the Barbour jacket and the woolly hat. He took the shotgun and dropped in a couple of shells, clicked it shut and checked the safety.

"Okay Alex, lock the door, keep the lights off, and don't open this door for anyone unless it's me or the kids." Lance

Corporal Brennan was back in full force. He flicked the light off, gave his eyes a moment to adjust, and stepped out into the yard. He made his way down to the first gate and climbed over the top. He headed out towards the edge of the field, and along the side of the river, staying low and looking for the cottage up ahead. The lights were on, and there was music coming from inside. He reached the back of the cottage and could see Rone and Sofia dancing to the music from the radio. He made his way to the side of the building and there, next to the shed, was some cover. He could see the front and the back of the place from here; anyone approaching had to come across the field, so, at some point, they would be silhouetted against the lights from the farm. No way they were coming through the river. He settled back into the cover, the gun resting in the crock of his arm, his thumb ready to nudge off the safety. Where had he done this before? Where indeed.

He'd become adjusted to the night and breathing through his nose down into the jacket so his breath would not be seen. He could hear the kids laughing; the back door opened and light flooded out. Rone came across to the woodshed, stacked some wood in a small basket and shouted back to Sofia. "Here, Mrs Farmer Giles, don't you go burnin that there toast, or you'se is just gonna have a plate a beans!"

He could hear Sofia laughing in the background, "You've made deformed toast again!"

Rone was oblivious to the fact his dad was mere feet away. The cold ate at him but Harry knew he had to remain still, perfectly still and become a piece of the background.

Grimaldi thought it was time. He'd walk back along the road and see if he could find a way in without crossing the farm. He had two lengths of cord in his pocket, the switchblade and a snooker ball tied into a long sock. He stepped out of the car and pulled on a dark jacket; he hated the fucking countryside, always cold and damp.

As he closed the car door, he heard a car coming along the road. He backed in behind the tree; anyone passing may see the reflection of the lights, and they'd probably think it was a couple shagging. He pressed back. The car passed, and then slowed quickly; he couldn't see it from behind the tree, just make out the lights. It stopped, and he heard the whine of the gears as it reversed back along the road, he couldn't risk a look. But, it wasn't a car, it was a police van.

"Eye, eye, what's all this then?" Dog van muttered. "We'd better take a look at you. That's a London registration if I'm not mistaken." He pulled the van into the gateway behind the Vauxhall and looked for his torch. It was on the floor amongst sandwich wrappers and a half-eaten pork pie. He picked up the torch and was momentarily tempted by the rest of the pie. "Later," and with his usual struggle, he was out of the van.

He shone the light into the car. "Hmmm, keys in the ignition…bit careless." He'd have a look. Grimaldi let him open the door, and as he bent to look inside, Grimaldi stepped out and plunged the knife into the back of his neck, just at the base of his skull. 'Dog van' barely twitched.

Grimaldi was struggling to pull off his police coat. He had his way into the farm and the cottage, didn't need to go walking around in the mud and shit.

Chapter 18
Dog Van

Parky had gone to the cells under the station. "Any free, mate?" He asked the booking sergeant. "Sure, mate, let me grab you a couple of blankets." Parky was too tired to go home, he just wanted an hour to shut out the noise. He'd been on the go for over 24 hours, and his brain was mush. He needed to think in straight lines, and right now it felt like the thinking part of his head was on some kind of slalom track. He'd left his guys sifting through the information looking for the 'victim' that may have a record or some possible link to any kind of London crew; they'd have to be known; maybe the break would come. They had to keep sifting.

Jacks had stayed in the office. After Harry's call, he was tempted to get the driver to take him up to the farm. He wasn't sure what he could do on scene, but it would be better than sitting here. They had to find Grimaldi. They had nothing; they'd hit any known leads. Singer had nothing on where he might be. He's like a fucking ghost.

He called back Bedfordshire police. "Anything at all at the farm? Have you sent anyone to check?"

"We've sent an officer down, he's going to call in and check and make sure." They'd sent a unit.

Was the officer alone? Yes, they were a bit short-staffed at the moment.

Jacks was drumming his fingers on the table: "You do realise how dangerous this suspect is?"

He dropped the phone back into the cradle, doubts running around in his head knocking over chairs, smashing plates and causing chaos.

"Where's Parky, had anyone seen him?"

"He's in the cells, Guv. He was dead on his feet; he's gone for a bit of a lie-down."

Time was getting on. If he got in the car now, he reckoned he could be at the farm in a couple of hours, by the time they got through the evening traffic. His hand rested on the phone, doubt did another loop around, smashing some more plates, did a couple of windows, and had a sit-down.

Where was the lad who'd driven the other night…Steve…He'd leave Parky to have a sleep; the boy was shagged out and no use if he can't think. No, fuck it, he'd go, can't let the local bods try and deal with this. He'd draw a sidearm, just to be sure. He made three quick calls: one to the lads who looked after the armoury, one to Irene, and the other to chase down Steve.

His phone was answered by a female voice.

"Steve, unless you've had some drastic surgery in the last day or so son, that ain't you."

The voice was all business. "He's in the canteen, drinking tea, and I have to answer his bloody phone."

"Very well young lady, can you tell him DI Jacks is looking for him?"

Her voice seemed to jump upright. "Sorry, sir, I'll go see if I can find him."

"No, don't worry, I'll find him. I need to get a cuppa."

Jackie had gone about her business. Paul had driven her to the office and then to a couple of appointments across the city. He'd watched her demeanour; it was as if someone had told her cat got run over. He couldn't fathom it all. Could Carl Nyman have been such an asshole? He'd checked through what information they had on Nyman, and the short report said they'd been married for nine years and had Sofia in the first year. Jackie was successful and driven to succeed in the publishing world. Nyman had been working his way up through the insurance firm. Then at some point, she'd had an affair with a woman who was their neighbour, seems she wanted to go play for the other team. Then they split, the girlfriend moved back to the US and as Jackie's company had an office there, she applied for a position and had left. Sofia was in drama school at this point. And Jackie had just switched her off, just like now; but where was the caring woman he'd seen the other day? Must be in there somewhere.

Steve was sat amongst some other officers drinking tea. Jacks was at his shoulder. "Steve, old lad, we need to go."

"Where to, Guv?"

Jacks looked at the others at the table and just nodded in the direction of the door.

Steve took a big slurp of tea. "Okay, Guv, coming."

One of the others at the table made a mooing sound and a crack about cow shit. It stopped Jacks dead in his tracks. He turned back. Steve's face was frozen, staring at the guy who'd made the noise.

"What did you say?" Jacks snapped. He banged both fists on the table making cups jump and spilling tea and coffee. He shouted directly into the officer's face, real 'hair drier' shout.

"What the fuck did you just say?" He had Steve by the front of his shirt, staring into the face of the other officer, his temper flaring.

Then turning to Steve, "Who else fucking knows anything else about fucking farms?"

Steve had gone as white as the tabletop. "Nuffin, Guv, was a joke. The lads saw me washing cow shit off the car."

Jacks glared at him and made his grip tighter. "You'd better not 'ave fucking told anyone where they are, or so help me, I'll lock you up in the Scrubs and tell all the fuckers in there you're 'old bill' son. You understand? Well, do you?"

He was eyeballing the other officer. "You'd better tell me what this fucking big mouth wanker said, son, or I'm gonna have your bollocks off."

The scene in the canteen was frozen. Other officers were staring at the table; had Jacks finally cracked? Jacks pulled them both out of their seats; he looked across and saw the custody sergeant.

"Go find Parky, wake his fucking ass up and get him to my office now! And I want these two grassing fuckers in separate cells." Other bodies came forward. "Get this fucker out of my sight!" He pushed Steve away. Suddenly chaos was back, smashing more furniture, and it would throw the TV out of the tenth storey window. Jacks had to assume that the hiding place was a bust. This place leaked information like a sieve, and something about the way Steve had acted…call it old copper intuition told him he was the leak. "Fuck, fuck, fuck!" He was on his way back to the office.

Grimaldi had rolled 'dog van' around and, although he was a fat fucker, he'd managed to get him sat in the seat of the Vauxhall. He'd got his coat off, pocketed the cuffs and was now wearing his coat. It was way too big, but in the dark, it just had to get him past the farmhouse. Fucking bumpkin farmer wasn't going to check. He checked the back of the van, no dog…hmmm, perhaps the fat fucker had eaten it? He backed the van out onto the road, drove along to the lane leading down to the farm, turned in, and slowly made his way to the farmyard. He opened the gate, swung it back and secured it open. He'd need to leave quickly, didn't want to be fucking about with gates now, did he? The outside lights were on in the yard and the front of the house.

The house was on his right, all the lights off inside; these farmer types turn in early. He was looking for some kind of place where they had put the girl: in the house here? He wasn't sure what to do, he stepped out of the van, pulled on dog van's hat and had a look around the yard. He could hear dogs barking inside the house. There was the briefest of shadows at a window. He'd been seen; time to act like local plod.

Alex had seen the van pull up in the yard; the officer stepped out and put on his cap. He seemed to be taking a long time to look around the yard, and now he looked directly at Alex. He stepped back from the window. Grimaldi zipped up the front of the jacket and made his way up to the door. He had the torch in his left hand, and the blade in the other, tucked inside the palm of his hand. He waved the light around looking for any reaction inside, but could just hear the dogs barking.

He did his best 'PC plod' knock on the door. Alex hovered on the other side of the door. The dogs were shut in the kitchen, perhaps he should let them out. What was it Harry had said? "Don't open the door unless it's me or the kids," but then he'd asked the London copper to send local police. This bloke must have just come to check.

"Hello, who is it?"

"Police, we're checking everything is okay. Is everything okay? Sir?"

"Yes, all fine, no problems."

"Is Miss Nyman okay?"

Alex was a bit surprised that he would know her name. "Who?" He asked.

"Miss Nyman, sir. It may be easier if you just opened the door, so I don't have to shout."

Alex reached up for the door catch and looked through the glass at the very top of the door. The policeman had his back to the door. Looking out into the yard, Grimaldi heard the door catch start to turn, and before Alex had it fully undone, he shoulder-barged the door. It flew open, knocking Alex off his feet.

Grimaldi was astride him. "Where are they? Where are they? Don't fucking piss me off!"

Alex had hit his head in the fall, his world was spinning, and he passed out.

Grimaldi smacked him hard, nothing. "Fucking bastard!" He was up and running up the stairs, banging doors open and turning on lights in the rooms. The place was a fucking museum, just one bedroom used, the others empty apart from some boxes and junk. She wasn't here.

Looking up, Harry could see lights from a car outside the house. They remained stationary, and he could just make out a figure walking in front of the light with a torch waving around. Jacks must have called the local police, and they were checking up. Fair enough. He stayed very still, keeping his position; he was really cold by this point. If it was the plod, they would be on their way in a moment; but the lights remained still. Doubt was having a chew at the back of his mind, and it was getting to the meaty part.

Grimaldi was back at Alex; he was barely conscious now. "Where are they?" He was waving the knife in Alex's face, "Where are they? I'll fucking cut you, do you understand? Tell me where the fuck they are!" He smacked Alex again and again, but he was too far gone to answer. "Fuck!"

The dogs in the kitchen were pounding paws on the door. The barking had reached a crescendo of noise; maybe they were in the kitchen? Dogs are a bit tricky; he reached in his pocket for the sock with the snooker ball. Alex was groaning away on the floor. He looked down, "Useless fucker!"

He went to the door. The dogs on the other side sensing their master wasn't there, leapt at the door again and again. Grimaldi had the sock raised; he'd need to hit hard and act fast. He pushed the door open a few inches and the dogs' noses snarled through the gap at him. One dog had a paw in the gap and was scrabbling to get out. He let the head come through and brought the ball down hard hitting the dog on the head. It yelped with pain and backed away. The other dog hesitated just for a second, and he pushed the door open and it came for him. He attacked it with the ball and the knife. The dog was silent, the room empty. They weren't here.

Jacks had Parky in the office. "Lad, we have to get to the farm. I'm going to call the local bods, make sure their man has been to check; but if that fucker has given away the location, Grimaldi could be there, and the locals have no idea what he's capable of." He grabbed the phone and dialled out for his contact in Bedfordshire. "Can you get a car arranged, Parky? Let's get going."

Grimaldi was back out the front of the house. Where were they? He saw the track leading down through a gate and walked down and looked over it. He could see a small place a few hundred yards along the track, the lights on, smoke from the chimney. "Gotcha!" He undid the chain on the gate and let it swing open. Back in the van, he wiped the blood from the dog on his trousers and drove down through the gate. They had to be there. He'd do the 'PC plod' act again to get in the cottage, and then he'd have plenty of time to put his plans for the girl in place.

Harry saw the car heading down the track. *That's odd, why would Alex have sent them down here?* He thought.

He shifted his weight slightly and eased back a little further into cover. As the car bumped its way along the track, the lights bounced around, but he was sure he couldn't be seen. He'd thought momentarily that he'd stand up and greet them, but a figure suddenly appearing out of the dark may just cause a mess. No, he'd see what this was. Could it be one of Jacks blokes? Let's hang back a second or two. As the car got to the front of the cottage, it turned across his view, and he saw it was a police dog van. It rattled some distant memories; when had he seen that? To be sure, they all looked the same. Couldn't be that fucker who'd told them about Rone? He shook the thought out of his head. The van had stopped, and the door was open. The kids were oblivious to the van arriving; they were washing up in the kitchen, the music up loud, singing along, Rone doing his best to sing along to 'London Calling' by The Clash.

Alex was aware of Sue licking his face. She was whining and pawing at him. The world went for a swim around, and he was struggling to move. He had to get up. He had to sit up and move his limbs. Harry and the kids were in danger. The phone, he'd got to get to the phone. If only he could move. "C'mon, you silly old bugger, c'mon." Sue was bleeding from her head, the blood running down her nose and onto the floor. "C'mon," he made a huge effort and the room swam again. "Sue, come, Sue." He saw the gash on her head. "Bastard!" He rolled over and pushed himself onto his knees. Sue came forward again to lick him, and he used her to stand as best he could. The sight in his left eye wouldn't focus, and he had his hand on the wall to balance. His one thought was to get to the phone.

Grimaldi was out of the van. He had the ball and sock back in his pocket and the knife palmed. He was swinging the torch by the strap, and he walked to the door. The music was up loud; he knocked hard on the door with the torch. Rone was dancing around the kitchen reaching the final chorus. Sofia singing along and they just heard the knock. Rone reached to turn down the radio, and there was the knock again. Rone looked at Sofia. "Can that be Alex? It's a bit late for him. Normally, he turns in early."

She made a little shrug with her shoulders. "Nobody knows we're here, apart from Alex and your mum and dad."

The knock at the door again, and just as Rone clicked the key round in the lock, the door flew open!

Harry was looking at the copper. He was pretty sure that was 'dog van' but there was something making him itch about the way he moved. He didn't have the rolling waddle that 'dog van' had, and somehow he didn't move right. His senses were up and alert. 'Dog van' was knocking on the door with the torch.

"Who knocks like that? Not a copper, for sure. He'd knock with his knuckles." The doubt was rattling around, but something had him stalled in place. He banged again with the torch; a few seconds later, the door opened and the 'copper' lunged forward.

Harry heard Sofia scream, and he was up moving with the shotgun raised, safety off. As he reached the door, he turned in and there was Rone on the floor bleeding from his shoulder, Grimaldi on top of him trying to snap handcuffs on him. Sofia was frozen by shock. She wasn't registering what was happening.

Harry had the gun in the back of Grimaldi's head. "Don't fucking move, not a finger. Sofia. Sofia, get a cloth, get it on that wound."

Sofia snapped back to the world, saw the gun, saw Harry and the moment reeled back and rushed her back into action.

Grimaldi felt the shotgun and he'd heard the demand. Rone was conscious and breathing hard. The wound in his shoulder oozed blood. Grimaldi had the knife to his throat.

Harry pushed again with the shotgun. "Take the knife away from my boy or I will fucking shoot you, you piece of shit."

Sofia stood to one side with a tea towel.

Harry spoke again. "Stand up!" He poked him hard with the barrel, knocking off the police cap. "Sofia, stand back until the fucker gets up off Rone."

Grimaldi's head was spinning up. He had to stand. This silly old fucker would shoot him, he felt sure. The boy was wriggling beneath him. He could cut him, make him bleed, and then the old man's attention would be on saving him. Would take the smallest move with the knife.

Harry tapped him again. "Get off my boy, get up!" Harry tapped again and Grimaldi moved his head to the side. Harry was about to lean in again with the barrel and Grimaldi's movement caught him off guard. The barrel went forward past Grimaldi's head, and as it came past, Grimaldi lunged with his left hand, caught the barrel and pulled it down. The shotgun went off with a deafening bang, and the buckshot rattled into the floor next to Rone's head!

Sofia jumped back. She was staring at Rone, at the gun, at Grimaldi, at Harry trying to pull the shotgun back. Grimaldi was up on his feet, lunging forward. He stabbed at Harry, the knife plunged into the Barbour jacket, but the jacket was baggy. He stabbed out again and again but wasn't reaching flesh. Harry had recovered. He pulled back with the shotgun and tried to back away, but Grimaldi kept coming, the long gun useless in the small room. Rone had rolled over, and was trying to get up, he was holding his ear. Sofia had the towel on his shoulder; the two kids were frozen on the spot. Harry was trying to get Grimaldi away as he slashed and stabbed with the knife. Harry dropped the shotgun so he had both hands free. Grimaldi kept coming forward and Harry stepped back to avoid the knife. He had to get control, but Grimaldi was a madman!

Rone reached down and picked up the shotgun. He was deafened by the blast next to his ear. He tried to focus, but his brain had taken a little sit down, it was out of breath and trying to recover. He tried to get Grimaldi into his sights, but with his dad ducking and weaving around Grimaldi, he'd shoot his dad. The two men were almost out the door.

"Shoot him, Rone!" Harry cried out, "Shoot this fucker!" Rone was in so much pain from the knife wound in his shoulder, and he could see his dad shouting but he couldn't hear.

Grimaldi lunged again with the knife; as he thrust forward, Harry managed to punch out and hit him square in the face. Grimaldi shook like a dog; he was lapping this shit up. They were out the door; he motioned Harry forward, Harry flashing looks at Rone. "Shoot, Rone, fucking shoot him!"

Sofia was motioning to Rone to shoot, but Rone couldn't see how he would not shoot his dad. He was frozen; his mind couldn't process what was happening quickly enough. He looked at Sofia; she was shouting and screaming. Where had he seen this before?

Grimaldi slashed out again with the knife and punched out with his other hand. Harry went backwards and stumbled. Grimaldi thought fast; it would only be a matter of seconds before the boy recovered and came out with the gun. Time to cut his losses. He was off running towards the farm. Harry was in through the door and had the shotgun from Rone, back out, he bought it up and fired at the shape running in the dark. The shot peppered the ground next to Grimaldi's right foot and caught him in the ankle. He ran on, the adrenalin pumping, he hardly felt that he'd been hit. He'd get to the Vauxhall and get away, time for her another day. Harry was moving forward, pulling the pistol from the pocket of the Barbour. He cocked it and fired, but Grimaldi was getting out of range. Harry was running and firing, but he couldn't keep the pistol stable enough to hit Grimaldi, and he was getting away.

Rone's world rushed back in, picked him up and gave him a shake. He had to help his dad and protect Sofia. He saw his dad bring the shotgun up and shoot. Harry dropped the gun and ran. He'd reached into his pocket, and Rone saw he had a pistol and was firing. He chased after his dad; his breathing was fucked, and he couldn't keep up.

Jacks and Parky were in a marked Rover SD1-'Jam Sandwich'. The driver had the lights and sirens going, they were flying through the traffic. The lad driving liked a good emergency or a chase, right up his street, quite literally!

They patched through to Hertfordshire and Bedfordshire. They'd have cars meet them and run 'point' to get the other traffic out of the way. Once they hit the M1, the driver had the V8 pounding along as fast as it would go. They topped out at 130mph, and the Grenada from Hertfordshire was flat pedal trying to stay in front.

Harry was running and firing, but Grimaldi was through the gate and into the yard. Now the pain in his ankle kicked in and slowed him up, and he needed to go to ground and take a moment. He could see Harry in the outside lights running up to the gate; he had the pistol up again, fired, and the bullet smacked the wall next to Grimaldi's head, showering him with bits of brick. He ducked back through a doorway into a bigger barn, full of cows. He climbed over the bars and dropped amongst them. They mooed, and those lying down were up on their feet. Grimaldi was shooing them away, pushing at the beasts to make them move. Harry was in the barn. He moved along the feed trough trying to see Grimaldi, the cows moving around disturbed, and Harry had the other clip into the pistol, bringing it up. He was trying to get a vantage point to see. He stepped up on the edge of the feed trough. Grimaldi was at the back rail climbing over. Harry fired; the bullet ricocheted off the metal rail, zipping into the air. Grimaldi dropped into the yard and ran towards the next pen. It was dark, he'd hide. That fucker can't have any bullets left.

The local police were speeding towards Park Farm, the two Ford escorts flashing through the lanes, sirens neeh naahing into the night. Jacks and Parky were off the M1. The Bedfordshire car running point had the address for the farm; they'd go right through and assist. There was lots of Tango, Foxtrot, Mike etc. static and 'Rodger beeps' coming out of the speaker in the dash.

Harry had the gun up; he was breathing hard. That fucker was here somewhere. It was then he heard the screams. Grimaldi had jumped the rail, and landed on Hector! Hector was up in a flash; shocked from his dreams of whatever it was that Hector dreamed of. He smashed his head back and forth. Grimaldi was caught between the head and the bars, and the force smashed him to the floor. He was struggling to stand, the bull pounding around the small pen, goring down with his head and horns and smashing into the cage on each side. Grimaldi slashed out with the knife, stabbing at Hector. The big bull was stamping and pawing at the concrete floor. He smashed Grimaldi's legs with his hoofs and then bore down on him with his horns. Harry was outside the cage, the pistol up, pointing at Grimaldi. He looked up: Hector was snorting and goring down, bucking in the pen. Grimaldi was pinned down, and the bull smashed back with his horns. Grimaldi's head was crushed, and Hector smashed away at the lifeless body, his full rage unspent.

Chapter 19
Final

Harry stood for a moment taking in the scene. Hector smashed away at Grimaldi, his body rag-dolled by the brutal power and weight of the big bull. Harry realised he still had the gun up and slowly he dropped his arm. He was suddenly aware of shapes moving around him and looked back to see Rone.

"Dad!" He was holding a blood-soaked towel to his shoulder. Harry reached out and put his arm around the now-shaking boy. Sofia had stopped to help Alex. The yard was suddenly full of lights and cars, doors slamming and voices shouting out. Rone was having several experiences all at the same time. He caught sight of Grimaldi, his dad, the pistol, and life took a complete loop. It was all too surreal; he really needed a smoke and a pint. He'd make do with holding onto his dad for a bit.

Shouts for ambulances and officers running with torches. A few seconds later, two more cars flew into the yard, and Jacks was out, calling out for Harry, Sofia, Rone. Sofia came out of the house, Jacks was with her straight away. "Harry, Rone?"

She pointed to the doorway through to the cows. "They went that way."

"You okay?" She nodded. She was white with shock. Officers bought blankets out the boots of cars and wrapped Alex and Sofia. Jacks was calling out for Harry, "Where are you?" He came through into the back of the cow shed. Harry stood in front of Hector's pen.

"Here, mate, we're here." Harry with the pistol in his right hand. Rone was with him.

Jacks looked at the pistol: "Better let me have that, Harry."

Harry looked down, seemed a bit surprised, clicked the safety on, dropped out the clip and racked the chambered bullet out.

"Don't want any silly accidents now, do we?" Jacks was reaching out, "Give it to me, Harry, please. And Grimaldi?"

Harry motioned his head behind him. Hector was nudging the lifeless body with his horns.

Jacks looked square at Harry: "Did you kill him or was it that bloody monster, mate?"

"He jumped in. City idiot probably thought it was a normal cow."

Jacks nodded and dropped the pistol in his coat pocket. The less said about that the better.

Ambulances arrived and they took Alex, Sofia and Rone to the hospital in Bedford. The wound to Rone's shoulder was cleaned and stitched. Sofia was checked over, no physical harm, and she was in Rone's treatment cubical when Jacks found them.

Rone looked up at him. Jacks looked shattered.

"You okay, lad?"

"I'll live. Is it over? Is the madness over? Co's I'm not sure we can do much more of this."

Jacks nodded. "He's gone, mate, we've closed down a lot of the people responsible."

He looked at Sofia. She looked incredibly vulnerable, and he wasn't sure how he was going to tell her the next part. So much of her life had been torn apart. He looked at Rone and looked back at her. "What is it, inspector?"

"Sofia, I'm sorry, but your father is dead. I'm afraid the man who was trying to get to you killed him last night."

Her facial expression barely changed, but she shook and tears rolled down her cheeks. Rone swung around off the treatment bed and was kneeling at her feet. He put his hands in hers and sank his head into her lap.

Harry was with Alex. He'd got a serious concussion. They had to keep him in.

"Who'll do the milking, Harry? Who's gonna look after the farm?"

"Don't worry, Alex, I'll get it sorted."

"What a mess. Did they get the body back from Hector?"

"Yes, his blood was up, and they couldn't get near him. So they called out the vet to dope him up a bit. They hooked the remains out, and Hector was snoozing off the effects. No harm to him. Grimaldi was almost unrecognisable; Hector had smashed him to pulp."

"Is it over, Harry? No more nutters going to show up, mate, eh?"

No, he didn't think so. He'd wait for Jacks. They needed to give statements and so on. The local police and the Met wanted everything squared away. He needed to go and call Chrissy and Nick and let them know what was happening.

"And Sofia, did they tell her about her dad?"

"They have, Alex. She's in pieces; don't know how they'll get out the other side of this."

Parky had headed back to London. The two forces involved agreed to one set of statements, and they would be done in London in the next couple of days. Parky had to get it arranged. He also had to sort out that low-life bloody driver, and find out who it was who'd told the mob where the kids were. There was a shit ton of work to do, and they still had the lead to chase on the bomb. He'd find out tomorrow what the others had discovered; he was beyond tired and as the Rover whistled its way back down the M1, he was asleep by the time they passed Toddington services.

A week after Christmas, they had a break in the bombing case. The suspect they were looking for amongst the victims had turned out to be a known member of a London gang. They identified him from fingerprints taken from a hand found in the pub. The gang had been involved with a gold heist at Heathrow some time back, and the bomb was intended to blow a hole in a wall of a bonded bullion building to have another go. They arrested a suspect who was going to be the driver and he gave up the bomb maker, and there was the sting in the tail: who'd made the device? Seemed Sapper Bob's thoughts about RDX and the device being simple but effective were true, and Bob's mate Johnny had got himself in financial scrapes and needed money to pay off some gambling debts and some loan sharks.

And once arrested and charged, Johnny gave up the rest of them.

Bob had gone to see him. "Why, mate, you could have come to me. I ain't got much, but I'd have dug in. Why bombs for wrong'uns, mate? What's all that farking about? And RDX, where did that come from, Johnny?"

"Ah yeah, it came from some artillery shells that were supposed to be destroyed on the range. Truth is, I'm dying, Bob, ain't got long. They can lock me up for life; it'll be about three months. I doubt I'll make the trial."

"But thirty-two people, Johnny…farkin hell mate…thirty-two lives, you silly old fucker. Why hand it over in a pub, for fuck's sake?" It was and wasn't Johnny's fault.

Seems that the bloke handling the bag had been a bit clumsy. When Johnny left him, he'd ordered a pint, went to the toilet. When he came back, he banged the bag down on the top of the stool and initiated what in the explosives trade was called a 'sympathetic detonation'. Not very sympathetic for the poor buggers in the pub, and as Bob had said after, "Who the fark hands over a farkin bomb in a bag, in a pub full of people? It's the sort of stupid that gets people killed!"

It took some weeks to tidy loose ends up in the Nyman case. It was going to be a long road to the trials of those involved. Farina had vanished; they couldn't find any trace of him. Interpol had him as a top priority.

Parky looked across the desk. He hadn't had a request for tea for at least an hour. Was the Guv sick, did he need a doctor?

"Ha bloody ha, lad, I'll let you know when it's time for a brew."

"How's Harry and the family, Guv, have you heard from him?"

"He's alright; he's back on the road after looking after Alex's place for a bit."

"Cor and what about that bull, what was his name…"

"Hector? Right as ninepence, lad, waiting for cow shagging season I expect."

Parky smiled away, "Ha, lucky old Hector, at least someone's getting some."

Just at that point, Alisha popped her head around the door. "You ready?"

Parky looked up and smiled. "Ready as I'll ever be."

She smiled back. "Make me a rolly, will ya?"

Parky popped open the tobacco tin, and duly obliged. He passed the cigarette across and Alisha flicked a lighter, lit the roll-up, and took a long drag on it. She made eye contact with Parky and flashed him another smile. "Shall we go?" She motioned towards the door, and Jacks looked at them both one at a time. Parky winked at him. "You never detected that, did you, Guv?"

He was waiting for her to leave the university building. He sat on the bike in the parking lot: the spring sunshine warming his face, the open helmet, dangling from the mirror on the handlebars. He checked the time on his Hamilton Emerson watch. He had on his much-loved 501s turned up twice, a white t-shirt and Vans; co's he was learning to skateboard and had found out what they were for. He'd lost the Harrington but got what the Americans called a windcheater. His self-confidence was rolling around on a beach enjoying the sunshine; self-doubt had been drowned in a flood during the Christmas holiday!

Seems Jackie wasn't such a cold emotionless hard ass. She had arrived the day after the mess at the farm and taken complete control of everything. It may have seemed a bit late, but it was time she took Sofia under her wing, time for a new start, and where Sofia went, Rone went. So when she found her a place teaching theatre studies at Monterey Bay University, she found Rone a place, working and studying at the Monterey Wildlife Sanctuary. Being very powerful in the publishing business had its advantages. She knew people, who knew people. He was among the animals and learning about the sea, it seemed to be his element.

She'd set them up in a small wooden house overlooking the ocean near Pacific Place. They'd received money from Carl's estate; they bought a pick-up truck, a motorcycle and found some peace. It had been a few months, and 1981 seemed to be rolling them towards being as happy as they could be, given everything that had happened. Sofia hadn't gone back to the theatre; her nerves needed some time to recover. She was teaching at the arts centre at the university, and it made her laugh because most of her students were older than her, but that meant they had a great social life with kids their age. It gave her the space and time she needed to recover.

She'd been diagnosed with a thing called PTSD. There was new research and there was hope that it could be treated. They'd both looked at the doctor with questioning eyes, "Post-traumatic stress disorder...?" And, as it had been the way of the last few months, they had each other, and their version of counselling was one of love and care for each other. Rone had a gentle soul. She had kindness and an open heart; they both had love and respect for each other.

"Here she comes," he took a beat; she was so beautiful. She was smiling at him, swinging her bag in her hand. The Californian sun had given her a warm glow to her skin, the blond hair still very short. She had on white shorts, a pale blue skinny T and her legs were tanned. She bounced as she saw him; she reached out put her hands on each side of his face and kissed him. She leant back and pulled off the Ray Bans; her eyes were as blue as the ocean and just as deep. He thumbed the starter, she hopped on the bike; he waited as she put on the helmet.

"Beach?" He asked.

She hugged her arms around him. "Sure, and I expect you're hungry, so, burger and fries on the way?"

He snicked the bike into gear, rolled the throttle and they headed for their favourite spot.